YANKEE GIRL

★

Yankee Girl

MARY ANN RODMAN

Farrar Straus Giroux ★ New York

For my parents, Roy and Frances Rodman

Special thanks to Sharon Darrow, Marion Dane Bauer, Ron Koertge, and Randy Powell at the Vermont College MFA in Writing for Children Program for their support and guidance; to Roy Rodman and Marion Turner for sharing their memories of the era; and to Craig Downing, Frances Rodman, and Shannon Rodman Blazek, my patient and faithful readers.

Copyright © 2004 by Mary Ann Rodman
All rights reserved
Distributed in Canada by Douglas & McIntyre Ltd.
Printed in the United States of America
Designed by Nancy Goldenberg
First edition, 2004
1 3 5 7 9 10 8 6 4 2

www.fsgkidsbooks.com

Library of Congress Cataloging-in-Publication Data

Rodman, Mary Ann.
  Yankee girl / Mary Ann Rodman. — 1st ed.
     p.   cm.
  Summary: When her FBI-agent father is transferred to Jackson,
Mississippi, in 1964, eleven-year-old Alice wants to be popular but also wants
to reach out to the one black girl in her class in a newly-integrated school.
  ISBN 0-374-38661-7
  [1. Race relations—Fiction.   2. School integration—Fiction.   3. Schools—
Fiction.   4. Friendship—Fiction.   5. Civil rights workers—Fiction.
6. African Americans—Fiction.   7. Mississippi—History—20th century—
Fiction.]   I. Title.

PZ7.R6166Yan 2004
[Fic]—dc21   2003049048

YANKEE GIRL

★

1

FBI AGENTS FIND MISSING CIVIL RIGHTS WORKERS
Bodies Found in Dirt Dam

★"Hey, kid. Look what I've got," shouted the mover from inside the van.

I whipped around to see him walking my bike down the ramp. I rushed over and grabbed the handlebars. I would check later to see if the movers had scratched or dented or in any way damaged my precious bike, Blue Rover. Right now, it was my ticket away from Mama, who was in one of her moods on account of us moving to Mississippi. I didn't even run into the house for my transistor radio. Usually, I didn't go anywhere without my transistor. You never knew when you might hear a Beatles song.

I ran Blue Rover down the driveway, put my left foot on the lower pedal, threw the other leg over the seat, and pumped away. Getting on my bike that way drove Mama nuts. I didn't care; I thought it looked neat, like a cowboy leaping on a horse.

Mama glanced away from the furniture on the sidewalk as I whizzed by.

"Alice Ann Moxley, where do you think you're going?"

"Exploring," I called without looking back. Time to check out my new territory.

I pedaled hard for about four blocks. It was hot. Really, really hot. Much hotter than in the house. Chicago sizzled in the summer, but the Lake Michigan breeze took the stickiness out of the air. Not here. Not the slightest whisper of a breeze. I inhaled thick, syrupy air that smelled of pine sap and cut grass. My legs felt heavy and my head started to spin. Maybe I'd better slow down. Maybe I should go back to the house.

I pictured Mama yelling at the movers. I pictured how much stuff was still in the van for Mama to yell about. I kept pedaling. Only slower.

Besides, this was my chance to make some friends. We moved a lot because of Daddy's job, so I was used to making new friends every couple of years. I never missed my old friends, because I figured I'd never see them again. They'd forget about me and I'd forget about them. That's just the way things went. I'd find friends here. No sweat.

I just had to meet them first.

Although it was ten o'clock in the morning, there was no one out and about. In Chicago, kids would be riding bikes or playing Barbies on the front steps. I didn't see a soul except a white-haired Negro man pushing a lawn mower.

I stopped short. Negroes lived far, far away from white

people in Chicago. You only saw Negroes downtown at the museums or waiting for the El train. Not in your own neighborhood.

I thought about the headline I had clipped from the newspaper at the motel that morning. FBI AGENTS FIND MISSING CIVIL RIGHTS WORKERS; BODIES FOUND IN DIRT DAM. Last year, my fifth-grade teacher made us keep a current-events scrapbook and I still did. These days my father, an FBI agent, *was* current events.

The FBI sent Daddy down South to protect black people who were registering to vote. White Mississippians didn't want black people voting, or doing a lot of other things that white people took for granted. Negroes had separate schools and public rest rooms and water fountains.

" 'Separate but equal' my foot," said Daddy. We were watching the news one night in Chicago. Walter Cronkite was talking about Negroes being arrested for sitting at a lunch counter in Mississippi.

"How come those people don't want to eat with Negroes?" I asked.

"It's complicated, Pookie." Daddy sighed. "Part of it is that Negroes look different. And that white people used to own Negro slaves. Some whites think they are better and smarter than black people."

"Isn't that why we fought the Civil War? And the North won!"

"And the South will never forgive us," said Daddy with a sour smile.

What a dumb idea, white people thinking they were better than black people. But that was all Down South, far away from me. It wasn't my problem.

Then we moved to Mississippi. Suddenly, it *was* my problem. And I was scared.

The trip from Chicago to Jackson, Mississippi, took two whole days. Daddy had the car radio on all the way. I hoped for the Beatles, but no. Daddy punched the radio buttons from one newscast to the next as each faded away. For a long time the news was all about the Ku Klux Klan burning down Negro churches and killing civil rights workers. I knew all about the Ku Klux Klan from Walter Cronkite. They wore white robes and hooded masks and hated Negroes, Jews, and anybody else who didn't agree with them. Hated them enough to kill.

"Would the Klan hurt us?" I asked.

"Don't you worry, Pookie." Daddy patted me on the head as if I were five instead of eleven. "The Klan won't get near the Moxleys."

By Memphis, we didn't hear any more about the Klan or bombings. Instead we heard about "outside agitators, stirring up the colored."

"What's an outside agitator?" I asked.

"Anybody who thinks that Negroes have a right to vote." Daddy gripped the steering wheel until his knuckles turned white.

"I guess that makes us outside agitators, huh?" I said.

"Let's talk about something else, shall we?" said Mama in a

tight voice. Somewhere between Chicago and Memphis a new wrinkle had appeared on Mama's forehead.

Eventually, our car sped past a sign: WELCOME TO MISSIS-SIPPI—THE HOSPITALITY STATE. I held my breath, waiting for KKKers in their pointy hoods to leap out of the dark and shoot into the car. Daddy glanced at me in the backseat.

"If anybody asks, you tell them your daddy works for the federal government," he said. "But only if they ask twice."

Now, in this morning's blazing sun, I shuddered, remembering the tone of his voice. Could anything bad happen in such an ordinary-looking place? No hooded men. No burning crosses. This neighborhood didn't seem that different from my old one in Chicago.

It was awful quiet, except for the *put-put-put* of the lawn mower. Then, in the distance I heard . . . girls chanting? I headed toward the sound.

At the end of the block, I saw five girls in shorts and sneakers, lined up on a driveway. They appeared to be about my age.

A bony-looking blonde stomped back and forth, yelling like a drill sergeant. "Straighten up, Cheryl."

A tan girl with a pixie haircut threw back her shoulders.

"Gum out of your mouth, Debbie." The blonde pointed to the ground.

Debbie was short and had a ton of hair ratted way high. "Who d'ya think you are? A teacher or something?" She had the thickest Southern accent I had ever heard outside of the movies.

Closer up, I could see that the blonde had a pointy nose and matching chin. She jerked that chin at Debbie's pile of hair. "Maybe you think you're so cute, we can't do without you. Is that it?"

"Maybe," said Debbie, as if "maybe" were two words. She went right on chomping her gum.

"Aw c'mon, Saranne," said a tall girl, her brown hair flipped under in a pageboy. "Quit acting like it's such a big deal. It's just cheerleading Hi Y football."

The blond girl, Saranne, folded her arms over her flat chest. "All right for you, Mary Martha Goode," she said. "You think you're so tough because, because . . ." Her voice trailed off.

The tall girl, Mary Martha, gave her a *so-what?* look.

"I'm hot," whined Debbie. "My hair is falling down."

I caught the eye of a redhead on the end. Aha! My chance to be friendly.

"Hi, you guys," I called with a big arm wave. I was all ready to ask them if Paul McCartney was their favorite Beatle, and if they thought his girlfriend Jane Asher was cute. Everybody liked Paul.

Saranne's eyebrows pushed up to her bangs. "You *guys*?" she repeated as if they were swear words. "I'm not a *guy*." She looked around at the other girls. "Y'all hear a Yankee round here? I think I heard a Yankee."

"I'm not a Yankee." Whatever that was.

"Y'are too," drawled Debbie. "Just listen to you."

The girls all giggled. All except Mary Martha.

"Oh, quit picking at her," said Mary Martha. She turned to me. "A Yankee's anybody from up North. Where you from?"

"Chicago," I mumbled.

"'Fraid you're a Yankee then." Mary Martha didn't look unfriendly. She looked curious.

"Well, Yankee Girl." Saranne tapped her sneaker toe on the driveway. "If you're all finished, we have to practice." She made a big deal of turning her back to me. "Ready? Let's do 'Turn on the Radio.'"

The girls popped into line like they'd been booted in the butt. They stood feet together, knees locked, hands on hips, chests thrust out. At least Mary Martha and Cheryl had chests; Saranne and Debbie and the redhead did not.

"Ready? Hit it," barked Saranne.

The girls jumped sideways and yelled:

Turn on the radio
Whaddya hear?
Elvis Presley doin' a cheer
You gotta F-I-G-H-T
F-I-G-H-T
You gotta fight, fight, fight
For victory
Yay!

Debbie was the best. She could kick high, leg straight, toe pointed. Saranne was pretty terrible. She couldn't get her legs higher than her waist and they bent at the knee.

"That was great," panted Saranne. I couldn't imagine what bad looked like. "Let's do 'Pork Chops.'"

That sounded interesting, but finding shade and water sounded better. I felt balloon-headed and wobbly-kneed. As Blue and I shoved off from the curb, Debbie yelled, "Let's do 'Bye-Bye Yankee Girl.'"

What went wrong? Usually I'd say, "My name is Alice, what's yours?" and I'd have a new friend. These girls didn't even give me a chance. They didn't know I loved Nancy Drew books, hated math, and was the president of the Beatles Fan Club at my old school. Oh well. Maybe things would go better once school started.

The road home was all uphill. I gave up pedaling and walked Blue home. The closer I got, the slower I walked. My hair sprang away from my face in damp coils, like bedsprings. My mouth felt gluey. I needed water, but the moving van was still in our driveway.

So was Mama, waving her arms at two movers carrying the sofa. I stopped at the yard next to mine, looking for a place to hide before Mama could spot me. The neighbors' pine tree had branches that drooped almost to the ground. I crouched under it, pulling Blue after me.

"Hey there," said a boy's voice. "Who you hiding from? You look like a scared bunny."

I jumped up, raking my fingers through my hair. They caught in a frizzy snarl over my left ear. No matter how much Dippity-Do I used, my hair just wouldn't lie straight and smooth like Jane Asher's.

The boy didn't seem to care that I looked like ten miles of bad road. He was my age, I guessed. Exactly my height, which was good. Last year, the fifth-grade boys only came up to my nose. He had big brown Paul McCartney eyes and light brown hair cut in a swoop of bangs over his forehead, short above his ears and in back. Not a Beatle haircut, but not a crew cut either. Only goobs had crew cuts. He was tanned, but with freckles across his nose and chipmunk cheeks. He wore a faded blue button-down shirt, sleeves rolled, tail hanging over madras shorts that had been washed until the colors bled. On his feet, scuffed loafers without socks. A silver ID bracelet rested just above his left wrist, but I couldn't read the name on it.

"You the new girl next door? I hear y'all are Yankees," the boy said. "Yankee" sounded nicer the way he said it.

"I guess. We're from Chicago."

"That's Yankee country all right." The boy looked me over, then stuck out his hand. "I'm Jeb Stuart Mateer." He paused. "I was named for the Confederate general Jeb Stuart. He's some kin to us."

I had never heard of Jeb Stuart, Confederate generals not being a big subject up North. I wasn't sure what "kin" was, so I said, "That's nice," wiped a damp palm on my shorts, and shook hands. "I'm Alice Ann Moxley."

"You go by both names?" said Jeb Stuart Mateer. "Alice Ann?"

"Just Alice. What do they call you?"

"Jeb. What grade you in?"

"Sixth."

"Me, too. Go to Parnell School." Jeb tossed a pinecone from hand to hand.

"Funny name for a school." I wished I had a pinecone. My hands felt big and floppy with nothing to do. "Up North the schools are named for presidents or trees or Indian tribes. My old school was named Potawatomi."

Jeb blinked. "Pota-*what*-omi? You think Parnell's a funny name? Schools round here are named for dead principals. I think Miss Parnell used to be the principal of our school." He pitched the pinecone at a streetlight. He missed.

"What happened to her?"

"Died, I reckon."

"So who's principal now?"

"Some new guy. Mr. Tippytoe, or something like that."

Jeb cracked his knuckles, one at a time. I rang my bike bell a few times to fill the silence. Between the pine needles, I could see Mama giving a moving man what-for.

"You and your mama fussing." Jeb wasn't asking; he was telling me.

"Kind of. She didn't want to move," I said. "All that stuff on the news. People getting shot at and blown up." I was scared, too, but I'd die if anyone knew.

Jeb wrinkled his nose. "Yeah, but those are civil rights people. The ones that want nigras to vote? Y'all ain't civil rights people," he went on. "Your daddy's an FBI man, right?"

"How do you know that?" I was afraid to find out.

Jeb shrugged. "Shoot, everybody knows everybody's business round here. But like I was saying, the FBI's different. They ain't a bunch of crazy civil rights workers bossing us around."

While I was happy to know that Jeb didn't hate FBI agents, I scarcely heard him after he said that *word*. I figured I'd hear it a lot down South. Just didn't think I'd hear it from the first person who was friendly to me.

"Don't you call colored people Negroes?" I said. "That's what we call them in Chicago." Already Chicago seemed ten million miles away.

"That's what I said." Jeb's round brown eyes were question marks. "Nigras."

"No you didn't. You called them niggers. That's not very nice."

Jeb's face cleared. "Oh! You thought I called them *niggers*. I said *nigras*. I reckon you ain't used to the way we talk. Nobody but white trash calls them niggers."

Those two words sounded pretty alike to me, but I was willing to take Jeb's word for it.

Next door, the movers wrangled Mama's sideboard through the carport. Even from across the yard I could see a big scratch in the side. So could Mama.

Jeb tugged my elbow. "Let her yell. It's eleven o'clock. Near lunchtime. You want a pimiento cheese sandwich? By the time we're done, she'll be over her hissy fit."

Any kind of sandwich sounded great, so I parked Blue in Jeb's carport and followed him in the kitchen door. A blast of freezing air shocked my sweaty skin into goose bumps. Air-conditioning, I reminded myself. No one I knew in Chicago had an air-conditioned house. Mama hadn't even figured out how to turn ours on yet.

"Brought company for lunch, Mama," Jeb said to a woman standing at the breakfast bar. She was all dressed up in a yellow knit suit, yellow flowered hat, and yellow high heels. She pulled on a pair of white gloves, while a teenage girl in white shorts and sneakers drew Mrs. Mateer's mouth on with coral-colored lipstick.

"This is Alice Ann Moxley." Jeb hoisted himself onto a tall stool.

"Hold still, Mama," said the girl. "You're smearing your mouth."

"Hey there." Mrs. Mateer blotted her lipstick with a tissue. "You the new girl next door? Name's Moxley? Any kin to the Moxleys from Corinth?"

By now I'd figured out that "kin" meant relatives, so I said I didn't think I was, since I had never heard of Corinth, except the one in the Bible. I was pretty sure she didn't mean that one.

Mrs. Mateer laughed and patted her hairdo. "That's right. I forgot y'all are Yankees." She pulled a can of Aqua Net from a pink purse the size of a mail pouch and gave her head a couple of quick blasts. "I'm off to bridge club," she said. "There's pimiento cheese and colas in the refrigerator, and chips in the cupboard. Don't call me unless the house burns down. Make yourself to home, Alice Ann." With a click of high heels on linoleum and the lingering smell of hair spray, she was gone.

The girl in the white shorts looked me up and down. After a morning of bike riding, I felt sweaty-nasty next to her. And young. With her white lipstick and eye makeup, she had to be at least sixteen.

"That's Pammie." Jeb knelt on the breakfast bar and dug into a cabinet. He emerged with a can that said Charles Chips and hopped down. Potato chips in a *can*? "She's in the seventh grade and a cheerleader. She thinks she's it with a capital I."

Seventh grade? Seventh graders down here wore lipstick and eye goop?

Pammie wrinkled her nose and waved her arms. "Rah, rah, rah."

"Alice is in sixth grade, too." Jeb rooted around in the refrigerator. "Pammie, did you drink the last Nehi?"

"What if I did?" Pammie flipped her perfect hair over her ears.

"Mama'll have a hissy, you drinking her grape Nehi's."

"See if I care. It's not like there isn't a Tote-Sum right down the road."

Jeb pulled bread and a Tupperware bowl from the refrigerator. "Anybody goes to the Tote-Sum, it ain't gonna be me. I went last time."

I opened my mouth to tell Jeb that there was no such word as "ain't" but didn't. I was learning that things were different in Mississippi—a lot of things.

Pammie pried open the Tupperware and scooped out a perfect mound of something orange with her knife. You just knew that she did everything perfectly. I bet she had perfect handwriting, never erased holes in her math workbook, and that her hair looked as perfect in the evening as it did when she took it out of jumbo curlers first thing in the morning.

"So, Mary Alice," she began.

"Alice Ann," Jeb corrected her. "'Cept she don't go by both names." He stuck a finger in the orange stuff and popped it in his mouth.

Pammie thumped Jeb on the head with the knife handle. "Mama catches you sticking your nasty old fingers in the food, she'll wear you out. So, Alice, you met anybody round here yet?"

"Just got here last night," I said, helping myself to what I guessed was pimiento cheese. This didn't look like Kraft Pimiento Cheese Spread. This looked . . . lumpy.

"Y'all have pimiento cheese up North?" Pammie watched me pick the lumps out with my knife.

"Yeah, but it doesn't look like this," I admitted. "It's smooth. Comes in a silver package from Kroger's."

"Oh, that's store-bought cheese," said Pammie. "Inez made this. Today's her day off, so she always leaves us food."

"Who's Inez?" I mashed the leftover lumps into the bread. I didn't care who made it; I didn't like lumpy food.

"The maid," said Jeb around a mouthful of Charles Chips. He caught my surprised look. "Don't y'all have maids up North?"

"Not anybody I know. Only rich people have maids."

"Well, everybody round here has one. Mama says as long as nigras work for nothing, she ain't about to scrub her own floors," Jeb said.

Pammie nibbled around the edges of her sandwich. "There's lots of sixth graders in this neighborhood," she said. "A lot of nice girls. I'm sure you'll like them once you meet them." Pammie sounded like somebody's mother, trying to be polite and interested when she really wasn't.

"I did meet some girls this morning, sort of." I took a bite of sandwich. This slimy, lumpy stuff didn't *taste* like Kraft Pimiento Cheese Spread, either. "A Cheryl and a Mary Martha and a Debbie and some other girl. Saranne?"

"How did you meet *them*?" Pammie looked interested now.

I told her, and as the story went on, she looked less and less impressed.

Pammie frowned. "Those will be the most popular girls in the sixth grade."

"Oh yeah?" said Jeb, digging into the potato chip can. "I think they're a bunch of drips."

His sister ignored him.

"I hope you didn't make them mad," she said.

"I don't think they care one way or the other about me." I shrugged. "They're not the only girls in the sixth grade."

Pammie looked serious. "You better hope Saranne Russell likes you, or you're going to have one long year in the sixth grade. Those girls have power."

"Oh, lay off." Jeb flicked potato chip crumbs at Pammie. "Sixth grade is the greatest. We're boss of everything. You couldn't mess up sixth grade if you tried."

I looked back at Pammie.

She just shook her head and repeated slowly, "One long year."

2

CITY SCHOOLS TO INTEGRATE
School Opening Delayed

★Mississippi was hotter than hot. Kids hardly ever went outside, unless they were biking down to the Tote-Sum for ICEEs. So Jeb and I played a never-ending game of Monopoly we left set up in the Mateers' freezing den. That was how I met Inez.

Jeb had been at my house, looking at my stamp album. "I didn't know girls collected stamps," he said.

"They do in Chicago," I said. "I like American stamps best. Lots of history stuff on them. Social studies is my best subject."

Jeb wrinkled his nose. "You can keep that old history stuff. I like the foreign ones. Come on over and see. We can play Monopoly after."

At the Mateers', a tall coffee-colored woman in a white uniform stood at the kitchen counter, mashing something in a mixing bowl.

"Y'all wipe your feet," she said without turning around.

"Inez, you got eyes in the back of your head," griped Jeb, but he went outside and wiped his feet. Me, too.

Back in the kitchen, Jeb boosted himself up on the countertop and peered into the mixing bowl. "Pimiento cheese!" he said, sticking a finger into the bowl.

The Negro woman batted his hand away.

"Mr. Jeb, you just take your nasty self offa my clean countertop," she said. "Then we can talk about some pimiento cheese."

"Sure thing." Jeb jumped to the floor and opened the bread drawer. "Alice, you want a pimiento cheese sandwich?"

"No, thanks." I watched Jeb slap together a lumpy orange sandwich.

"How 'bout a soda?" He poked his head in the refrigerator. "RC or Nehi? We got Sunrise orange, too."

"Sunrise, please." I waited for Jeb to introduce me to Inez, who was now getting herself a glass of water at the sink. But Jeb was busy with the bottle opener. Finally, I tapped her arm.

"Excuse me," I said. "I'm Alice Ann Moxley from next door." Mama would be proud I remembered my manners.

The woman turned around, looking startled. Then an almost smile tugged at the corners of her mouth.

"Well, Miss Alice, you must be the Yankee girl I've heard about. I am Inez."

"Pleased to meet you, uh Missus . . ." What was her last name?

Again, the woman looked surprised, before she said, "Green. Inez Green."

"Nice to meet you, Mrs. Green," I said.

A funny look flickered across her face. "You just call me Inez, like Mr. Jeb and Miss Pammie do."

I wasn't supposed to call adults by their first name. It was disrespectful.

Jeb made a rude sound. "Here, take your Sunrise." He thrust the open bottle at me. What was eating him?

"Hold the phone there, Mr. Jeb," said Inez Green. "You ain't drinking soda outta the bottle like trashy folk. Get you some drinking glasses."

"Oh, all right," he grumbled. "You're as fussy as Mama." He plunked down a glass tumbler from the cabinet, poured his Nehi, and wandered off to the den.

"Mr. Jeb don't have no manners." Inez shook her head.

"It's okay," I said. "Boys up North wouldn't even think of pouring your soda for you."

"Let me get you a glass," said Inez, reaching into the cabinet Jeb had left open.

"That's a pretty one," I said, pointing to a purple tumbler.

"I'm sorry, Miss Alice, but that one is mine. I brought it from home."

Why would she bring her own drinking glass? The Mateers had a cabinet full of glasses.

"Hurry up out there, will ya?" Jeb called from the den.

So I hurried into the den. Jeb sat cross-legged on the floor, watching the Three Stooges on TV, eating his sandwich. He looked away from the screen when he heard me come in.

"I know you don't know no better, so I'll tell you. First off, you don't introduce yourself to nigras."

"Why?" I put my glass down on the coffee table and plopped on the couch.

"I don't know," said Jeb. "It's just the rules, okay? And you don't call 'em Mister or Missus. You call 'em by their first name."

"But she called you *Mister* Jeb and me *Miss* Alice. That doesn't sound right."

"Does to me." Jeb took a slurp of Nehi.

"But why?"

"Because that's the way it's always been," said Jeb, sounding annoyed.

This discussion was going nowhere fast, so I asked the question I meant to ask Inez.

"How come Inez brings her own drinking glass from home?"

Jeb thumped open his *International Stamp Album.* " 'Cause she ain't supposed to use our glasses. She has her own plate and silverware, too."

"But *why* isn't she supposed to use your eating stuff?"

Jeb looked confused. "I don't know. She just does. All the maids do. They ain't supposed to eat off the white folks' plates and stuff."

"But *why*?" Was Jeb incredibly dense or what?

"I don't know." Jeb sounded mad now. "That's just the way

it is. That's the way it's always been. Now, do you want to see these stamps or not?"

"Yeah. Sure."

Mississippi was turning out to be one weird place.

Every day I discovered something new about living Down South.

I learned the Negro grass-cutter didn't live in my neighborhood.

"He's a yard boy," Jeb told me. "Lives over in Tougaloo with the rest of the nigras. Works for nothing. Good thing. I hate cutting grass."

Each day was hotter than the one before. There wasn't any place to swim. The city had closed the public pools rather than integrate. I flipped through my current-events scrapbook. Yep, there it was: MISSISSIPPI POOLS CLOSE IN FACE OF INTEGRATION. When I cut that out of the *Chicago Tribune* three months ago, I felt sorry for those poor kids burning up down South, with no swimming pools. Now *I* was one of those poor kids.

I learned about city buses.

"A bus stop right on our street," I told Jeb. "Neat! I can go downtown by myself."

"Are you crazy?" Jeb looked downright shocked. "Only nigras ride the bus. The bus stop is so's the maids can get to work. Buses ain't for white people."

I learned that Daddy was never going to be home. At least not while I was awake. It was a rare night that he ate supper with us. I couldn't go to sleep until I heard the Chrysler pull into the carport. When he was really late, I worried. What if somebody shot him? Or the Klan kidnapped him?

When he *was* home, Daddy acted strange. I'd always hugged him when he came home from work. Now, if I was up when he arrived, he brushed me off.

"Give a man a chance to change his shoes," he said, then went straight back to his bedroom. I could hear the door lock click, then drawers and doors open and close. In a couple of minutes he was back, his suit replaced with a sport shirt and sloppy pants.

"How about that hug now?" he'd ask.

Why did he have to change clothes to hug me?

Just another weird thing about Mississippi.

It seemed like Daddy worked all the time. Not that I saw that much of him in Chicago during the week. But Saturday was our special day, when Daddy took me for my allergy shots.

I used to cry about those shots, until Daddy taught me "the mind trick" when I was little.

"You know how Shari Lewis on TV makes Lamb Chop and Hush Puppy talk?" Daddy said. Dr. Davis stood by patiently, needle in hand.

"No," I sniveled.

"It's a trick called throwing your voice. Shari Lewis throws her voice so it just seems like her puppets are talking."

"So?" I quavered.

"So, what if you could throw your mind someplace? Then you'd be there and not here getting a shot."

"Like where?" I swiped my cheeks with the backs of my hands.

"Anywhere you want, Pookie." Daddy smiled, eyes crinkling behind his horn-rimmed glasses.

"Disneyland?" Only rich kids went to Disneyland.

"Why not?" said Daddy. "Or Niagara Falls, or the White House to see the President. You pick."

"Disneyland." I squeezed my eyes shut and pictured the opening of *Walt Disney's Wonderful World of Color* on our black-and-white TV. Tinker Bell shooting over Sleeping Beauty Castle, trailing sparkly fairy dust.

"You can have your sucker now, Alice," said Dr. Davis.

I hadn't felt a thing! It was a handy trick whenever I found myself someplace I didn't want to be.

Now Mama took me to Dr. Warren for shots. He didn't have Saturday office hours. Not that it mattered; Daddy worked seven days a week.

"It's just until things settle down," he explained.

"When is that going to be?" demanded Mama.

"I don't know," sighed Daddy. "Bombings, shootings, church burnings. The Klan is keeping busy."

Mama jerked her head my way. "Let's talk about this later." Like I didn't know what was going on from Walter Cronkite. Mama watched Walter Cronkite, too. Only she got up and checked on supper during the bad news.

I hadn't run into Saranne and her bunch again, which was okay with me. I had Jeb. We had lots in common. Monopoly. Stamp collecting. The same favorite TV shows. He wasn't crazy about the Beatles, but I could overlook that. Someday I *might* need a boyfriend. But until then, Jeb was my new best friend.

I told him so as we hiked down to the Tote-Sum one afternoon for ICEEs.

Jeb looked away. "Gee, Alice. I've been meaning to tell you." He kicked a pinecone ahead of him in the road.

"Tell me what?"

"Well, uh . . . I can't talk to you at school. Least not when anyone's around." The pinecone skittered into the weeds by the roadside.

"Why not?" Suddenly my stomach hurt. "Is it because I'm a Yankee?"

Jeb grinned. "Heck no. I don't care if you're a Yankee. It's 'cause you're a girl."

"I've always been a girl. How come it's bothering you now?"

"My friends Skipper and Andy, they've been gone all summer and . . ."

"And I was good enough to hang out with while they were gone," I finished for him. "All right for you, Jeb Stuart Mateer." I took off, my sneakers raising puffs of road dust.

Jeb caught up and snagged me by the elbow.

"Now, hold on. You didn't let me finish," he panted. "You're okay, for a girl. It's just that guys don't have girls for friends."

"So we're still friends . . . just not when anyone's around?"

"Yeah." Jeb sounded relieved. "Now you've got it!"

It was stupid, but I got it.

There was so much I *didn't* get. Living in Mississippi was like living in a foreign country. Jeb's accent was hard to understand. He could make three syllables out of the word "on." He called adults "ma'am" and "sir." No one talked like that up North.

Then there were the other neighbors. We never saw them. Not one person came over to say "Welcome to our neighborhood."

Only Mrs. Mateer was friendly. She'd come over and visit while Mama ironed. She perched on the den couch, shoes kicked off, feet tucked under her while she smoked. Mrs. Mateer never left home without her cigarettes and lighter.

"Why don't you have a girl do your ironing, like I do?" Mrs. Mateer flicked her lighter.

"A girl?" Mama wrinkled her brow. "You mean Alice?"

"You are a caution!" laughed Mrs. Mateer. "I meant a nigra maid, like Inez."

"But Inez isn't a girl; she's a grown woman." Mama flapped a blouse across the ironing board and dampened it with water from the sprinkler bottle.

"Oh, that's just what we call nigra women down here. Don't mean nothing by it. Why, Inez is like family. Anyways"—she waved cigarette smoke away from her eyes—"Inez is always looking for work for her kinfolk."

"No, thank you," said Mama, not looking up from the blouse. "I enjoy ironing."

That was a big, fat lie. How many times had Mama said, "Lord, I hate ironing. I'd rather scrub toilets."

"Suit yourself." Mrs. Mateer shrugged. "Sometimes Inez *is* more trouble than she's worth. I almost let her go last week."

Mama thumped down the iron. "Really? Why was that?"

Mrs. Mateer blew smoke out of her nose like a lady dragon.

"Some nigras was on the local news, registering to vote. I could've sworn I saw Inez signing up, bold as you please."

"Was it her?"

"She *said* not. I let it pass. I've had Inez since Pammie and Jeb were babies. I don't want to have to train up another girl."

A tiny steam cloud hissed from the iron.

"What if it was Inez?" asked Mama. "Doesn't she have the right to vote?"

Mrs. Mateer's smile was all teeth and lipstick. No friendliness.

"Nigras have no more notion who to vote for than Jeb."

The vein on Mama's forehead bulged, the way it did when she was upset. She changed the subject.

"So," said Mama, "when does school start down here?"

I guess all that talk about getting a "girl" to do the ironing got Mama thinking about the "girl" she already had. Me.

"It's high time you learned to do some of the housework," Mama announced one Saturday morning. She shoved the steam iron around a tablecloth, pausing to shift the pressed part down and the wrinkled part up.

"Hmmmm." I sat cross-legged on the floor, watching cartoons and eating Cocoa Krispies from the box. Outside I could hear Daddy wasting a rare Saturday off, mowing the lawn.

"I mean *now*, young lady. Put that cereal box away and come over here."

I did as she said. Mama got on these housework kicks now and then. She'd spend so much time showing me how to do something that she usually wound up doing it herself.

"You need to learn to iron." Mama showed me how to funnel distilled water into the steam chamber and set the temperature dial. She showed me how to dampen clothes with water from a 7-Up bottle with a sprinkler top.

"Why do you do that?" I asked. Not that I cared. Maybe if I asked enough dumb questions she would lose patience and do the ironing herself.

"A little water helps smooth out the wrinkles." Uh-oh. Mama thought I was *interested*. "Let's start with something easy." She poked around the laundry pile until she found a wad of plain white cotton squares. Daddy's handkerchiefs.

"Why don't we do yours?" I asked. At least Mama's were pretty, with lace and embroidery.

"They're too easy to scorch." Mama flapped a wet white square across the board. "Now, watch me."

Ironing was even more boring than I expected. Press the hanky out flat. Fold and press again. Fold and press again. All the corners had to match up exactly. I must have re-dampened and re-ironed each one four times.

A million hours and a crick in my neck later, I finished. All that work for a little stack of folded linen. No wonder Mama hated ironing!

"Nice job, Alice," said Mama. "Now, if you would put them away for me, you can go play."

I looked around Mama and Daddy's room, wondering where Daddy kept them. I started at the top of his dresser, yanking out drawers. Nope. Shirts. Nope. Socks.

I pulled open the middle drawer.

A gun in a holster was nestled among Daddy's undershirts.

A rattlesnake in the dresser couldn't have shocked me more.

I slammed the drawer shut. I knew that Daddy carried a gun for his job, but I had never seen it. He had always left it at the office.

"Guns don't belong in a house with children," he said, when I asked him once.

But that was years and years ago. Up North.

In Mississippi, Daddy had a gun in his undershirt drawer.

That's why he didn't let me hug him when he came home from work.

He didn't want me to feel the gun holster.

He didn't want me to know.

We needed a gun in the house.

In Chicago, school always started the day after Labor Day.

But not here. Not this year.

Daddy came in one night and tossed the evening paper onto the breakfast bar. "The Jackson schools are being integrated. School won't start for another two weeks," he announced. He pointed to the newspaper headline.

Terrific! In two weeks, I would own *all* the Monopoly properties, a new world's record, I was sure.

Mama slammed the oven door on the pot roast. "You didn't know about this any earlier?" she said.

"I did not." Daddy sounded annoyed. "The school district has been fighting integration all summer. They just lost their last court appeal, and now they need time to get ready."

"Ready for what? Should we be worried?" Mama nervously flapped the oven mitts against the kitchen counter. "Will it be safe for the children?"

Images from the news flashed before my eyes. Police dogs. White hoods. Burning crosses. My stomach did a cartwheel. That headline was about *my* school. Something that was going to happen to *me*. Now *I* would be part of current events.

"Look at the trouble those Negro children in Little Rock had," Mama pointed out.

"That was seven years ago," Daddy said. "Civil rights leaders have learned a thing or two since then."

"Such as?" Mama folded her arms across her chest.

"Such as avoiding confrontation. The parents will probably keep their children home a few days until all the fuss dies down. That won't stop the protesters, but maybe they'll get tired of it after a while."

"Why do Negro kids want to go to a white school?" I asked. "Schools are all pretty much the same, aren't they?"

Daddy shook his head. "Negro schools are mostly old and

falling apart. They get the white kids' leftovers. Old textbooks. Broken equipment. Beat-up desks. Wouldn't you rather go to a shiny new school with all the advantages, if you had the choice?"

My school in Chicago had been shiny-new. I couldn't even imagine one that wasn't. I wondered what Parnell School would be like.

I found out the following Wednesday, when our mothers took Jeb and me to register.

"How come you had to register?" I asked Jeb as we walked up the school steps. "You went to school here last year."

Jeb shrugged. "I don't know. Mama said everybody has to register whether you're new or not. Bet it has something to do with the nigras coming to school."

I blinked in the dim hallway, my eyes adjusting after the bright outdoors. I breathed in and relaxed. Parnell School was somewhere between falling apart and shiny-new. It smelled the same as my school in Chicago. Like the green soap in the bathrooms, sweeping compound, and pencil shavings, all mixed up with last year's vegetable soup.

We passed the office where the custodian was fastening a nameplate on the door that read PRINCIPAL BENNY THIBO-DEAUX.

"I'm going in here to see about transferring your records," said Mama. "Why don't you go with Jeb and meet your new teacher?" She disappeared into the office.

I nudged Jeb. "Is that how you spell Tippytoe?" He shrugged.

32

Mrs. Mateer turned her head. "It's a French name," she said. "Young fella from downstate, I heard."

We passed a poster-painted banner: WELCOME TO OUR SCHOOL. The last two letters of "school" crawled sideways up the end of the paper.

"Second graders." Jeb's lip curled. "They mess up everything."

"Sixth grade, right here." Mrs. Mateer hustled us into a room labeled 6A.

I stopped dead in my tracks. Hanging over the chalkboard were three flags. The American flag, one that I had learned was the Mississippi state flag, and a . . .

"Is that a rebel flag?" I whispered to Jeb, pointing to the third flag. "What's that doing there?" Up North, we learned in social studies that the rebel flag stood for evil slave owners who seceded from the Union. I sure never thought I'd see a rebel flag in a schoolroom.

"It's the Confederate flag," Jeb corrected me. "It's a symbol of our glorious heritage." I could tell he had heard some adult say that.

What glorious heritage? I started to say. *You guys lost the war.* But I decided that might not be the smartest thing to say to a boy named for a Confederate general.

A young woman with perfectly flipped silver-blond hair sat at a long table covered with cards and papers. She looked up at Jeb and me standing in the doorway.

"Y'all come on in." The woman smiled like we were the best thing that had happened to her all day. "I'm Miss LeFleur. In French *la fleur* means 'the flower.'"

It seemed like a good name for her.

She wore a madras shirtwaist dress, penny loafers, and silvery pink lipstick. She couldn't be a teacher; teachers weren't this young and pretty.

"Are you the new sixth-grade teacher?" asked Mrs. Mateer. "I heard Miss Carpenter retired."

"Yes, I'm taking Miss Carpenter's place." Miss LeFleur flashed a quick smile. She had dimples! "However, Miss Gruen is still here. She retires at the end of the school year." She handed Mrs. Mateer a sheaf of papers. Miss LeFleur's fingernails were painted pink; her silver charm bracelet tinkled faintly. I hoped that I would get Miss LeFleur and not some cranky old teacher who was tired of sixth graders.

"Where is Miss Gruen?" Mrs. Mateer fanned herself with a registration card.

"She's . . . uh . . . at a meeting at the Central Office." Miss LeFleur suddenly found something fascinating in a stack of papers.

"This wouldn't have anything to do with that integration business?" Mrs. Mateer asked sharply.

My insides squirmed. Was there going to be trouble after all?

Miss LeFleur shuffled through her cards, bracelet jingling. "Please keep your voice down." She dropped her own voice to a whisper. "Some colored girls are coming to school here. I really can't say more." Her nostrils flared, as if she smelled something bad. It was an ugly look on a pretty face. Then it vanished as quickly as it had come.

"Any of them going to be in the sixth grade?" Mrs. Mateer clicked open her purse and pulled out a gold fountain pen.

Miss LeFleur turned about six shades of red.

"It doesn't matter to me," said Mrs. Mateer, her pen moving across the registration papers. "Nigras have to go to school somewhere. I just don't want any trouble, know what I mean?"

I think I knew what she meant. I felt sorry for these Negro girls, whoever they were. Last Wednesday, during my visit to Dr. Warren, I had gotten a taste of how it felt, not being wanted.

"You Yankees," shrilled Dr. Warren's nurse. "Y'all come down here thinking you can tell us what to do with our nigras." She waved the patient information form, where Mama had written "FBI Agent" next to "Spouse's Occupation." Everyone in the waiting room put down their magazines and stared at us like we were Martians. "Why don't y'all go back where you came from? There's plenty of crime up North. Ain't none of y'all's business how we treat our nigras."

I tried to disappear behind a copy of *Life*, but it didn't work. Waves of hate came right through the magazine. These people didn't even know me.

I cringed at the memory as I watched Miss LeFleur paging through the registration cards. "Yankee, Yankee, Yankee go home" her charm bracelet jangled.

But I *was* home. Mississippi was home now.

3

CITY SCHOOLS OPEN TODAY
Race Mixing Plan in Effect

★"Ninety degrees here at Rebel Radio on this back-to-school morning," shouted the deejay on Pammie's transistor as Pammie, Jeb, and I waited for the bus.

The Dippity-Do on my bangs oozed down my forehead. Even though I wore a sleeveless dress, I felt like I was melting into the soft asphalt. The full skirt had a scratchy petticoat that prickled my waist and the back of my legs. My feet were swelling, hot and heavy in suede oxfords and ankle socks. Next to Pammie's short blue linen shift and dyed-to-match pointy-toed flats, I looked like a big, fat baby. Pammie even wore nylons!

"Does everyone wear nylons?" I asked.

"Not until junior high." Pammie rooted around in her purse. "Sixth graders wear Peds when it's hot. You know, those little shoe-liner things that just cover your foot? Don't girls wear Peds in Chicago?"

Some girls did. Girls with reputations.

"Mama wouldn't let me go without socks if it was two hundred degrees," I sighed.

Pammie pulled a tiny bottle out of her purse, unscrewed the cap, and took out . . . a toothpick? She offered me the bottle.

"Soak 'em in peppermint oil. We aren't supposed to have them in school."

"Okay." I might be dressed wrong, but I could chew the right thing.

"I'll take one of those." Jeb snatched the bottle from Pammie's fingers. He wore his usual madras shorts.

"You're allowed to wear shorts to school?" You sure couldn't do that in Chicago.

"Yeah, but only when it's over ninety. And only the boys. The schools ain't air-conditioned." Jeb gnawed his toothpick. "Whew, Pammie! How long did you soak these things? My head's coming off." He rolled his eyes and passed me the bottle.

"Don't get your hands near your eyes," Pammie warned. "Peppermint oil stings like crazy."

It stung my mouth, too, like candy fire. Once my sinuses stopped hurting, it tasted pretty good, though.

The school bus groaned to a halt in front of us. The door clanked open. I followed Pammie and Jeb on.

"Remember," Jeb muttered out of the side of his mouth. "Don't talk to me unless I talk to you first. Okay?"

"Okay." It wasn't, but I couldn't do anything about it.

"No toothpicks on the bus," said the driver, a teenager whose name tag said RALPH. "Ditch it."

I dropped the toothpick in the little trash can at Ralph's feet and faced my first problem of the school year. Where to sit?

I spied Saranne and the Cheerleaders in the rear seats, giggling about something. No room there. I scouted around for Mary Martha. She hadn't been friendly, but she hadn't been mean either.

Mary Martha wasn't on the bus.

Jeb fell into a seat across from a redheaded girl. Nope, not with Jeb. I wasn't even supposed to talk to Jeb, let alone sit with him.

Pammie plopped down next to a girl reading a *16 Magazine*, and turned the transistor up full blast. The Beatles' "Hard Day's Night." So much for Pammie.

"Siddown, kid," yelled Ralph. "No standing."

The bus lurched forward as I swayed down the aisle, looking for a seat.

"Turn down that radio," yelled a big scruffy-looking boy. "Stupid Beatles." He looked old enough to be in junior high, but the notebook in his lap said "Parnell Rebels." Maybe he'd flunked a grade. Definitely a goob.

The redheaded girl across from Jeb clouted the gooby kid with her purse. "Shut up, Leland Bouchillon. The Beatles are the fabbest." Braces twinkled on her upper teeth. I recognized her as the redheaded Cheerleader. A fellow Beatlemaniac!

"Can I sit here?" Before she could say no, I asked, "Who's your favorite Beatle?" And sat down.

"Ringo, of course. Everybody likes Ringo." I should have guessed. "Carrie loves Ringo" was scrawled in red Magic Marker across her three-ring notebook.

"Unless they like Paul better. I do," I said.

"Paul is just cute," the girl said. "Ringo has personality. You know you've got green goo on your forehead? Aren't you the Yankee?" She sang along to "Hard Day's Night," braces flashing. I dabbed at the Dippity-Do goo with a Kleenex. The tissue stuck to my fingers.

"Where's Mary Martha?" I asked when the song ended.

"She doesn't ride the bus," said the girl. "She lives across from school." She stared straight ahead at "Leland B stinks," scratched into the metal seat back.

I tried again.

"Is your name Carrie?" I pointed to her notebook.

"Whaddyathink?" She shrugged and looked out the window. At least she hadn't told me to get lost.

There was no air in the bus. All the windows were shut tight. I leaned across Carrie to unlatch the window.

"Don't do that," my seatmate said. "It'll blow my hair."

A dozen tiny smells grew into big smells in the hot, stuffy air. Hair tonic on the boys. Lime chewing gum. Peppermint toothpicks.

"Guess who's gonna be in our class?" hollered Leland, the gooby boy, bouncing in his seat. His flattop haircut stuck up in greasy spikes.

"Dry up, Leland," said Jeb from across the aisle. I glanced over at him, but he was talking to a boy with a crew cut seated in front of him.

Leland stood and yelled, "Doesn't anybody care who's gonna be in our class?"

"Siddown, Leland," hollered Ralph.

"Okay," sighed Jeb. "Go ahead. Tell us."

"Valerie Taylor," Leland announced.

Heads turned. Fifty pairs of eyes stared blankly at Leland.

"Who's Valerie Taylor?" said Carrie-the-Ringo-lover.

"Valerie *Taylor*?" Leland repeated. "Reverend Taylor is her daddy!"

Jeb gave a low whistle. "You're kidding!"

"Wow," said the boy with the crew cut.

"How do you know, Bouchillon?" asked someone from the front seats.

"I have my ways," said Leland with a smirk.

"Who's Reverend Taylor?" I asked.

Jeb gave me a boy-are-you-stupid look.

"You know, *Reverend Taylor*. Martin Luther King's right-hand man? *That* Reverend Taylor."

Reverend *Claymore* Taylor? I'd heard of him, even in Chicago. Whenever Martin Luther King marched or made a speech for civil rights, Reverend Claymore Taylor was always at his side.

"Bet there'll be TV reporters at school," said Jeb. "We're gonna be famous."

TV reporters . . . and what else? I knew from Walter Cronkite what happened when schools integrated. Jeering crowds, snarling police dogs, fire hoses turned on full blast.

"Don't see why the big fuss," grumbled Leland. "Jus' some nigger listening to Martin Luther Coon what thinks she can go to school with white kids."

"Hey, you can't call him Martin Luther— *Ow!*" A three-ring notebook smashed me in the head.

"Oops," said Jeb.

"What was *that* for?" I rubbed my scalp.

"You were fixing to say something about Martin Luther King, weren't you?" Jeb shielded his face with his notebook so no one could see him talking to me.

"Well, yeah," I said. "Didn't you hear what that Leland guy said?"

"If you want to get along around here, don't ever stand up for Martin Luther King or anybody colored."

"Why not?" I whispered behind *my* notebook.

"You just don't," Jeb said. "You don't have to say anything bad about him. Just don't say *anything*, okay? Unless you just *want* kids to hate you."

The bus took a sharp corner and there we were. Parnell School.

A mob of grownups swarmed over the playground and sidewalk. My stomach churned and my hands turned to ice.

So this is what it's like to be a current event. I'd rather read about it in the newspaper.

"Ooba dooba," yelled someone in the front seat. "Look at that!"

"Hey, are those TV cameras?" Saranne called from the back.

"Look at all the cops," added Crew-Cut Boy.

"Cool it, Andy," said Jeb. "You never seen a cop before?" Jeb sounded calm, but he looked a little white around the mouth.

"Oh boy," squealed Debbie. "We're gonna be on TV." She fished a lipstick from her purse and drew a crooked pink mouth as the bus jounced to a halt.

Outside, the crowd chanted, "Two, four, six, eight, we don't want to integrate!"

Nobody on the bus moved. Nobody made a sound. Ralph cranked open the door.

"Okay," he bawled. "All you Parnell kids, off."

With the bus doors open, the crowd sounded even louder.

"Send 'em back to Africa!" someone yelled.

"Y'all ain't scared, are you?" Ralph grinned. Ralph didn't have to worry. He wasn't getting off the bus.

"Eight, six, four, two, send 'em back to Tougaloo!" the crowd shouted.

"Y'all a bunch of babies? Get off the bus," ordered Ralph.

One by one, we stepped into the aisle. No pushing, no shoving, no tripping. As careful and polite as a film on bus safety. Andy, Crew-Cut Boy. Leland. Jeb. Then me.

Follow Jeb. Keep your eyes on Jeb.

I stared at the back of his blue shirt. A spreading sweat stain turned it a deeper blue.

"Niggers, go home! You ain't gonna marry my kid!" shrieked a woman's voice.

I stared down a human tunnel that stretched to the school

door: policemen, and reporters with cameras in the front row. Behind them, people shook their fists and waved signs that said SEGREGATION NOW AND FOREVER and NIGGER GO HOME.

The sign-wavers shouted words I couldn't understand except for "nigger" and "coon," their faces twisted with hate. I grabbed the back of Jeb's soggy shirt. I had to hang on to someone.

Beyond the crowd, a car horn brayed the first notes of "Dixie" over and over. *Oh I wish I was in the land of cotton.* Over and over.

The path narrowed as the cops struggled to keep the crowd away from us kids. Red screaming faces strained over the locked arms of the police.

Sweat trickled down my sides.

Keep moving. One foot after the other.

The front door was just ahead. Somewhere.

Remember Daddy's trick. Send your mind someplace else.

The Dunes. The Indiana Dunes at Lake Michigan. A lake breeze ruffled my hair. The scorching sidewalk turned to beach sand. The screaming mob faded into the surf slapping at the shore. I breathed in beach smells: Coppertone, hot dogs, and the slightly sour smell of lake water.

I opened my eyes. The shouting sign-wavers searched the line of kids for Valerie Taylor. Little by little, the noise died down as only white kids made their way up the front walk.

In the open school door a tall man in shirtsleeves waved to us.

"This way, students," he called. "Don't be afraid."

Jeb and I stepped through the door into the warm, dim hallway. Safe inside, I felt my legs suddenly turn to Jell-O.

"Let go of my shirt," Jeb grumbled. "You got it all wrinkled."

The tall man pointed toward the auditorium. Inside, teachers directed us to seats, one right after the other, as if they were parking cars.

"I don't sit next to girls," protested Jeb as Miss LeFleur waved us to our seats.

"You sit where you're told," snapped Miss LeFleur, not so sweet today. "And no talking."

The auditorium seats steadily filled, row after row. Kids craned their heads to see if the latest arrivals included Valerie Taylor.

Every single person in that room was white.

When it seemed as if the auditorium couldn't get any hotter, the shirtsleeve man climbed the stage steps and walked over to a microphone.

"Boys and girls, I am Mr. Thibodeaux, your new principal," he said.

Mr. Thibodeaux looked too young to be a principal. He had a lot of dark hair combed straight back with hair goop. He seemed like he might be nice. For a principal.

"Students," said Mr. Thibodeaux, "we are a part of history. Parnell is one of five city schools that will have colored students this fall."

"You mean niggers," muttered somebody behind me.

"Our new students will arrive in the next few days. I expect you to treat them as you would any other student. Do we understand each other?"

Silence.

"I said, do we understand each other?" The principal frowned and his eyebrows met in a straight line over his nose. "Say 'Yessir, Mr. Thibodeaux.'"

"Yessir, Mr. Thibodeaux," the room echoed.

"And now, students, let's begin the school year with the Lord's Prayer."

"You pray in school? Isn't that against the law?" I whispered to Jeb.

Jeb cut his eyes sideways but kept his head down. "Yeah, but only folks up North pay attention to it. Mama says folks up there are all atheists."

"But . . ." I started to tell Jeb that all Northerners were *not* atheists, when I caught a whiff of scent behind me. Yardley's English Lavender, like my grandmother kept in her nightgown drawer. A real old-lady smell.

The smell grew stronger as a pudgy, brown-speckled hand clamped on to my shoulder. It belonged to a toad-faced woman in a prune-colored dress.

"Hush your mouth, or I'll send you to the office," said Toad Woman.

"Amen," said five hundred voices, with Mr. Thibodeaux's, loudest of all, crackling into the microphone.

"You are dismissed to your classrooms. Let's have a good

year," shouted Mr. Thibodeaux as five hundred folding seats slammed shut. The toad-faced teacher turned her attention to the kids surging toward the door.

"Who caught you talking?" Jeb said as we inched up the aisle.

"Some teacher. Didn't you see?"

"Not me. I was praying." Jeb pulled an innocent face that somehow looked just the opposite. "Let's see whose class we're in. Now, don't get the idea I'm going to do this all the time," he added quickly. "Just today, 'cause you're new."

Kids stampeded past us, since there were no hall monitors yet. The girls all wore shifts and slip-on flats. Not one in a full skirt and oxfords. I felt like a freak. A sweaty, frizzy-haired freak.

We stopped at the door to room 6A.

MISS LEFLEUR'S CLASS, read the sign. WELCOME TO 6A. Bright construction-paper cutouts of fall leaves decorated the door.

Jeb and I scanned the blurry mimeographed list taped beneath the sign. We read it three times but didn't find our names.

"Miss Gruen, here we come," sighed Jeb.

There was no welcome sign on 6B. Just the list of names, with MISS EUGENIA GRUEN written in no-nonsense black Magic Marker across the top.

Jeb and I went in.

Behind the teacher's desk stood the Toad Woman from the auditorium.

Miss Eugenia Gruen. My new teacher.

"Hey, Yankee Girl." Someone goosed me from behind. I turned around. Saranne. "I hear Miss Gruen eats Yankee Girls for lunch. With salt."

Great. Just great. Miss Gruen *and* Saranne Russell.

It *was* going to be a long year, just like Pammie'd said.

Leland Bouchillon stomped in.

"Hey, did y'all see the list in the hall? That Valerie Taylor girl is gonna be in our room."

A very, very long year.

4

NO INCIDENTS REPORTED IN FIRST WEEK
OF SCHOOL RACE MIXING

★I snickered as I glued that headline into my scrapbook. Of course there hadn't been any "incidents" the first week of school. There hadn't been any Negro students. At least not at Parnell. Still no Valerie Taylor.

"Why do they call it 'race mixing'?" I asked. "The newspaper's always using that expression."

"It means the newspaper doesn't like the word 'integration,'" said Daddy. "They think it's too civilized a word for something they don't want to do."

Even without "race mixing," sixth grade turned out to be tougher than I thought.

If math was hard in Chicago, it was twice as hard in Mississippi. It was harder because I couldn't understand Miss Gruen's accent. Her words ran together like poured molasses. I raised my hand three times that first morning to ask what she'd just said. Not that it helped. I didn't understand the second time either.

"I don't know about up North, but here we expect students to pay attention," said Miss Gruen after the third time. At least I think that's what she said.

Then there were the Cheerleaders. They always looked like they were having fun. Giggling in the lunch line. Trading Beatles cards on the playground before school. Singing along to Debbie's transistor on the bus.

That is, until I showed up. Suddenly the smiles and giggles shriveled and died. They stared over, through, and past me. I felt invisible.

It's because I'm new. They'll just have to get used to me.

I hovered at the edges of the group, hoping that someday they would let me in on the fun, too.

The Cheerleaders were harder to figure than math or Miss Gruen. They weren't the prettiest girls in the class. Or the smartest. They just were. And they had *power*!

When Saranne announced that her favorite word was "vomitaceous," sixth graders used it in every other sentence. It wasn't even a word. I looked it up.

Debbie chewed *only* lime Fruit Stripe gum. Suddenly, *everybody* chewed lime Fruit Stripe. No one would be caught dead with orange or cherry.

Cheryl, Saranne, and Debbie decided that Paul was their favorite Beatle; the other Beatles were vomitaceous.

"I like Paul," I said, sidling closer.

"Anybody want to trade a John for a George?" said Saranne, as if I weren't standing right next to her. They were trading cards that came in packs of vomitaceous bubble gum from the Tote-Sum.

"I don't care," said Carrie. "I still like Ringo."

"Mary Martha, you never said which Beatle you like best." Debbie fanned her cards like a poker hand.

"I like them all," Mary Martha said with a polite smile.

"That's just plain ignorant," sniffed Debbie. "Everybody's gotta have a favorite. I'll trade a Ringo for two Pauls." Carrie and Debbie passed the cards right over my head.

Yep, Invisible Alice. That was me. Invisible most of the time: When I wasn't picked for kickball and Miss Gruen made a team take me. When the girls talked about sleepovers or going to the movies. When I sat in the front seat on the bus, because none of the sixth graders let me sit with them; nobody wanted to sit behind Ralph.

The more they ignored me, the more I looked forward to Valerie Taylor. *There* was somebody who *really* needed a friend. She wouldn't care that I was a Yankee.

On the third Monday of sixth grade, Valerie arrived.

The protesters and reporters and police still hung around, but not as many. I don't know how she got past them, but Valerie was already standing by Miss Gruen's desk when we came in.

"Class, this is Valerie Taylor." Miss Gruen stood behind Valerie, not quite touching her. "I know you will show her the same courtesy you would any other member of this class." Her expression added the "or else."

Valerie reminded me of the flagpole in the auditorium, tall and straight and thin. Freckles spattered her honey-colored cheeks and nose. I didn't know Negroes freckled. A reddish brown ponytail swooped down her neck like a feather plume.

"She don't dress like a nigra," Debbie said to Carrie, not bothering to whisper.

What did that mean? How were Negroes supposed to dress? I liked Valerie's maroon dress with the monogrammed collar.

"Mama says she don't trust a nigra that'll look you in the eye," Carrie said back. "Means they're uppity. Don't know their place. See, she's looking right at us."

No, she wasn't. Her eyes, the gray of a winter sky, looked *through* us, not at us. As if she didn't see us at all. Anyway, she sure didn't look like she wanted a friend.

"You may take the seat behind Leland," said Miss Gruen. "Raise your hand, so Valerie can see you." Leland sat catty-corner from me, the last desk in the last row.

"No nigger gonna sit behind me," Leland grumbled, but raised his hand.

Miss Gruen opened her roll book and began taking attendance, scanning the rows for empty seats.

Valerie moved down the aisle, eyes fixed on her new desk. Suddenly she sprawled in the aisle beside me, books flung one way, notebooks another. Leland jerked a sneaker back under his desk.

"What happened?" Miss Gruen didn't move, her voice cool as water.

"I tripped, ma'am." Valerie gathered her belongings without looking up.

Miss Gruen gave us all the fisheye but went on taking roll.

I leaned over to help Valerie. She smelled like Ivory soap.

Something sharp poked me in the back.

"Don't do that," Jeb hissed, pencil poised to jab again.

"Why?"

"Tell you later. Just don't!"

Jeb cornered me at recess as I waited my turn at kickball.

"You can't be helping that nigra," he said. "You know what kids are gonna call you?"

"Isn't Yankee Girl enough? What else could they call me?"

"A nigger lover. And no one will be your friend."

"Big deal," I said. "You're my only friend anyway." Then I got what he meant. "You mean if I talk to Valerie, you won't be my friend anymore?"

Jeb scuffed at a bald spot in the grass with his loafer. "You don't get it. Nigras ain't like us."

Miss Gruen yelled, "Alice Ann Moxley," and then a whole sentence I couldn't understand. Why couldn't Southerners talk normal?

"Huh?" I stepped up to home plate.

"She said it's your turn to kick," said Jeb.

Miss Gruen marched across the infield and grabbed me by the elbow. "Young lady, you say 'Yes, ma'am' and 'No, ma'am' when you speak to an adult. Didn't they teach you manners up North?"

I didn't know what to say, besides "Yes, ma'am."

Chicken hips! I was about to lose my one friend, and my teacher hated me.

I made the third out for our side.

"Nice going, Yankee Girl," Saranne yelled as we headed for the outfield. "Bet that nigra can kick better'n you."

Where *was* Valerie? From the outfield I spied her, slouched against the school wall, staring at her loafers. No one had picked Valerie for their team, and Miss Gruen hadn't made anyone take her.

An ear-shattering whistle split the air. Miss Gruen had our attention.

"Class! Time to go inside. Line up, please."

No one wanted to be next to Valerie. The kids on either side of her scooted away from her.

"Pee-yew, I smell something," said Debbie, who wasn't anywhere near Valerie.

"Niggers always stink," added Leland.

Halfway down the hall, we stopped at the water fountain. When it was her turn, Valerie drank, then daintily patted her mouth with a hanky.

Suddenly, the kids behind her in line weren't thirsty. I was glad when the rest of the class headed for the room, because I had a bad case of cotton mouth. But before I could even get close to the fountain, Jeb grabbed my arm.

"What do you think you're doing?" he said.

"Getting a drink of water. What does it look like I'm doing?"

"Not after *her*. Are you crazy?"

"But I'm thirsty."

"It's almost lunch. You can wait."

So! Jeb was my friend after all. He talked to me in front of his friends! He was right. I could wait half an hour for lunch.

We had assigned seats in the lunchroom. Saranne and Debbie and Leland, who chewed with his mouth open, sat across from me. Carrie and Andy, who had a retainer he liked to pop in and out with his tongue, sat on either side of me.

None of them talked to me.

"Hey, somebody pass me the salt," Saranne said. Carrie passed it right across my plate.

"Thanks, sweetie." Saranne's voice dripped sugar.

Why is she nice to everybody but me?

"Wonder where the nigra's gonna sit?" asked Andy.

"Who cares?" Leland said with his mouth full. "Long as it ain't with us."

"Look," said Carrie. "She's just standing there."

Valerie gripped her tray, eyes flicking around the room.

Miss Gruen appeared and hustled Valerie toward the teachers' table.

"She gonna eat with the teachers?" said Carrie. "I almost feel sorry for her."

"Feel sorry for the teachers, don't you mean." Leland crammed a roll in his mouth. "I couldn't eat with a nigger."

Miss Gruen pulled out a chair for Valerie at the empty table next to the teachers. After a few minutes, a smaller Negro girl joined her.

Valerie took a sip of water. The other girl picked up her roll, and then put it down, as if it were too heavy. They stared at their trays and ate nothing.

Lunch over, we lined up for the rest room with Miss LeFleur's class. Mary Martha, the girls' rest-room monitor, guarded the door, letting us in five at a time.

I punched the soap dispenser for a dribble of the green Lysol-smelling goo. Two girls from 6A strolled in just as Valerie came out of the toilet stall.

"Karla, look who's here," smirked the taller girl. "Miss Martin Luther Coon." She backed Valerie into a corner where the sink pipes met the water heater.

"I'm still hungry," said Karla. "I feel like some barbecue. Barbecued coon." She grabbed Valerie's wrist and forced it toward the pipes.

"Hey, you can't do that," I yelled without thinking.

"Says who?" said the tall girl. "You?" She spit out "you" like a bad taste in her mouth.

The rest-room door banged open. Mary Martha.

"Y'all get out of here before I write you up for talking," Mary Martha said, hands on hips, looking official.

The girls let Valerie go and slunk out, muttering about rat finks and snitches. Valerie smoothed her bangs, fluffed her ponytail, and left without looking at me or Mary Martha. Valerie Taylor was one cool customer.

Me, I was shaking all over.

"Thanks, Mary Martha," I said on our way back to class.

Mary Martha gazed at me, eyes clear and blue as a gas flame.

"The only reason I didn't write you up is you're new. I'll do it next time."

"Me? Who you need to write up are those two girls."

"Why?"

"They were trying to burn Valerie on the water pipes."

Mary Martha narrowed her eyes. "I didn't see anything."

"But you said you heard them," I sputtered.

"But I didn't *see* anything. It's your word against theirs." Mary Martha opened the door to 6B, and we went in.

All afternoon I tried to puzzle it out. I could be in trouble for talking in the bathroom, but not the girls who tried to burn Valerie?

I still hadn't figured it out by the time we filed to the coatroom before the closing bell.

Valerie's sweater was missing.

"Has anyone seen Valerie's sweater?" Miss Gruen's mouth flattened in a tight line.

The second hand on the wall clock whirred loudly in the silence.

"No one leaves until we find Valerie's sweater," said Miss Gruen.

Since half the class rode the bus, I figured Valerie's sweater would turn up in pretty short order.

It did.

"Look what I found." Debbie reached into the trash can under the pencil sharpener. Valerie's maroon sweater, dripping pencil shavings and bits of paper, dangled from Debbie's fingers. "Now, how did that get there?" She balled it up and threw it at Valerie.

Valerie calmly peeled the sweater from her face and shook the pencil shavings off.

Didn't Miss Gruen see Debbie? No, she was erasing the blackboard. She thumped the eraser into the chalk rail and turned around. "Class, line up for dismissal."

We lined up. The kids next to Valerie shrank away again. We were through the door and down the hall before the bell stopped vibrating. Outside school, we scattered like a bag of dropped marbles.

In all the commotion, I couldn't tell who knocked Valerie's books out of her arms. I did see Leland step on her sweater. On purpose.

Valerie picked up her belongings for the second time that day, and made her way to the curb where a white station wagon waited.

"I reckon Parnell is good and integrated now," Jeb said as we got on the bus.

I wondered if it would still be integrated tomorrow. If I were Valerie, I wouldn't come back.

I could see that making friends with Valerie Taylor would take some doing.

5

FBI ARRESTS THREE WHITES
IN HOME BOMBINGS

★*Br-r-r-i-ing.* The phone. I shot straight up in bed.

I hated phone calls after bedtime. They always meant trouble. A bombing, a shooting, a church burning. Or just someone telling us to take our nigger-loving selves back to Chicago.

Click. The light in my parents' room. Daddy. Mumble-mumble on the phone, his last words, "I'll be right there," like always. Thump. His feet hit the floor. Closet door creaked open then shut.

Daddy sock-footed down the hall. Clunk. He dropped his heavy-soled shoes by the back door to put them on. Back door rasped open and closed. Car door thunked shut. The Chrysler coughed, then whined into gear as it backed out of the carport.

Go back to sleep.

But I couldn't. I clicked on my transistor to see how many

far-off stations I could find. I got Cuba once. I think it was Cuba; the deejays jabbered in Spanish. I wished *I* were in Cuba, even if it was full of Communists. In Cuba, I wouldn't have to worry about the Ku Klux Klan. Or the Cheerleaders. Or Valerie.

Living in Mississippi was so confusing, it might as well have been Cuba. Even Mama and Daddy couldn't figure things out. For the first time, they didn't have all the answers.

"I don't know what ails these people," Mama said at supper one night. "Have some meat loaf, Alice. And some string beans."

"Hmm?" Daddy helped himself to mashed potatoes and passed me the bowl.

"The Negroes act so strange." Mama handed Daddy the gravy boat.

"How so?" Daddy ladled gravy over his potatoes.

"For one thing, when I walk down the sidewalk, they jump out of my way like I'm the Queen of England."

"Happens to me, too," said Daddy. "They're used to letting white people pass by. I've had Negroes step into the gutter to let me by."

"Well, I don't like it," said Mama. "It gives me the willies."

Daddy shook his head. "There's some things laws can change. Years of being forced to bow and scrape to white people isn't one of them."

"Another thing," Mama went on. "When I speak to a Negro man, he looks at the ground. I like a person to look me in the eyes when I talk to them."

"I'm not surprised," said Daddy. "They're afraid to speak to white women."

"More Southern stupidity." Mama plopped mashed potatoes on her plate.

"Not stupid at all," said Daddy. "Negro men have been lynched for talking to white women. Or even looking at them. Remember Emmett Till?"

"Who's Emmett Till?" I asked.

"A Negro boy from Chicago, not much older than you. He was lynched a few years back while he was visiting Mississippi. Supposedly, he whistled at a white woman. Didn't matter whether he did or not. Somebody *said* he did. White men took him out in the country, beat him, shot him, and threw his body in the river."

"That's terrible!" I put down my fork. "Did they catch those men? Was it the Klan?" I never thought about *kids* being killed by *adults* before.

Mama glared at Daddy. "Let's talk about more pleasant things, shall we?"

Daddy cleared his throat. "So, Alice. How's Valerie Taylor doing?"

That was his idea of pleasant?

"Okay, I guess." I took a bite of meat loaf. "The kids are kind of mean to her. But she doesn't act like it bugs her or anything."

Daddy gave me a long look over the top of his glasses. "Do you talk to Valerie?"

"I don't *not* talk to her," I said. "Not on purpose, anyway."

Daddy slowly sliced his meat loaf. "I'll have to think about that one."

"Well, it's hard! If I talk to her, then nobody will talk to me. She doesn't act like she wants to talk anyway."

"How can you tell?"

I skated a string bean around with my fork. "It's like she's a robot or something. She stands up for the Pledge and sits down for the Lord's Prayer and the rest of the time she stares at Miss Gruen."

"She's probably scared to say anything. I'll bet she's waiting for someone to break the ice. You, for instance."

There were things that parents just didn't get. Daddy would say that making friends with Valerie was the Right Thing to Do. There was the Right Thing and the Wrong Thing. No in-betweens.

"I'll bet you two would have a lot in common if you sat down and talked," Daddy went on.

"Hmmm," I mumbled into my milk.

"Just give it a try," he said. "I know you'll do the Right Thing."

End of conversation, thank goodness.

That night I dreamed that Valerie jumped off the sidewalk to let me by.

"Don't be silly," I said. "I'm just the same as you. We have a lot in common."

But Valerie had turned into a Negro boy.

"Who are you?" I asked.

"I'm Emmett Till," he said. "But you ought not to be talking to me, miss. Not where folks can see. It's dangerous. For both of us."

Daddy was right about one thing. Valerie and I did have something in common. We were the most unpopular kids in the sixth grade.

Everyone still called me Yankee Girl, except Jeb. *He* didn't talk to me at all if his friends were around.

"Nothing personal," he reminded me. "You know how it is."

Yeah, I knew how it was and I hated it. I hated Parnell. They did dumb stuff we didn't do in Chicago.

Like folk dancing.

On rainy days, we folk-danced in the auditorium instead of going outside for recess. There were lots of rainy days in October.

Miss Gruen put on a scratchy record of some old geezer calling "The Paul Jones."

"All join hands and circle left," hollered the caller.

I took Andy's sweaty hand, and turned toward a boy from 6A named Duane. He was picking his nose. Yech! I wasn't about to take his hand. I grabbed his wrist and circled left.

Valerie sat in the front row, reading a library book. No one would dance with her. For once, I envied her. I hated folk dancing.

As much as I hated folk dancing, I hated lunch more.

"It must be a hundred degrees in here," griped Jeb as we stood in the lunch line. "Why don't they open the windows?"

"They *are* open," I pointed out.

"Then how come it smells like old sneakers?"

"That's lunch," cracked Andy.

It was Roast Beef Day. Stringy roast beef, covered by a brown gravy skin. I collected my food and sat down.

Andy popped out his retainer and plunked it on his tray. Trying not to look at the pink plastic thing, I gulped down the least disgusting parts of lunch. Not a good idea. Because right after lunch was math. Math always made my stomach hurt.

On this rainy afternoon, I stared at my *New Directions in Math* workbook, while Toad Woman croaked directions.

"Put your workbook on my desk when you finish. Then you may have a free art period."

I tried to hurry through the assignment. The problems dissolved in a jumble of plus and minus signs, parentheses and brackets. The page became a gray smear with a hole erased in the middle.

I rubbed my eyes and stared out the window at an oak tree. The wet leaves looked like big cornflakes as they slid to the ground. Soggy cornflakes. Lunch rumbled in my stomach.

6B smelled even worse than the lunchroom. Leland never changed his shirt. Jeb was experimenting with his daddy's cologne. Today he wore enough Old Spice to flatten an elephant.

The smells. My stomach. I turned hot, then cold, followed by a sour taste in my mouth. I wobbled up to Miss Gruen's desk.

"I feel sick." I hoped I'd throw up on her teacher's edition of *New Directions in Math*. "Ma'am."

Miss Gruen peered over her steel-rimmed glasses. "You may go to the clinic in the office."

Ka-chung, ka-chung, ka-chung. Mrs. Messer, the school secretary, was running the ditto machine when I stumbled in. Usually, I loved the smell of ditto ink. Today, it was one smell too many.

"You sick, hon?" She felt my forehead. "You don't have a fever." A whiff of her inky hands, and my stomach lurched. I moaned.

"You going to throw up?" Mrs. Messer took a quick step back.

"I don't think so." Now that her hands were out of nose range.

"All right. But you can only stay a little while since you don't have a fever." She opened a door marked CLINIC and let me into a tiny closet of a room.

I kicked off my shoes and flopped across the nearest cot. A fan ticked in the corner, putting me to sleep. I woke up when the door clicked open. Mrs. Messer and Valerie stood in the doorway.

"There." The secretary pointed to the other cot, her mouth crimped in a mean line. "You best not be faking, girl." She left, thumping the door shut behind her.

Valerie placed her loafers neatly beneath the cot and unfolded the blanket at the foot. She stretched out, pulling the blanket over her shoulders.

At last, I could talk to Valerie without anyone knowing.

"Hi," I said.

Valerie stared at the ceiling.

I stared at it, too. Nothing up there except ceiling tile, the kind with little holes in it.

"Lunch got me," I said. "Did you eat the beef?"

Cot springs squeaked as Valerie settled in.

"It wasn't just lunch," I went on. "I hate math. My stomach gets all snarly. Do you like math?"

A sound from the next cot. I turned on my side to look. Valerie stared straight up, big tears sliding toward her ears.

"What's wrong?" I said. "Want me to get Mrs. Messer?"

"Leave me alone." Valerie flounced over, turning her back to me.

"Fine," I snapped. "I don't want to talk to you either. I wish I'd never heard of you or Parnell or Mississippi." I turned my back on *her*. Even Valerie wouldn't talk to me. Now my stomach *really* hurt.

"Don't talk to me," said a blanket-muffled voice. "Just 'cause I go to school with white kids don't mean I hafta talk to them. I never wanted to go to this sorry old school anyway."

"You didn't?" This was news to me.

"Shoot, no." I heard Valerie punch her pillow a couple of times, then flop back down.

"Then how come you're here? I mean, if you're not even going to try to be nice to white kids."

"Because my daddy said so. Didn't even ask if I wanted to. It's not fair."

"Me, too." I sat up. "I mean, nobody asked me if I wanted to move down South."

Sca-reech sang the cot springs as Valerie sat up. She cleared her throat. "Daddy keeps saying stuff like 'You're making history. You're blazing a trail for black children in years to come.' I don't give a horse's patoot about history. Let them kids blaze their own trail."

"My folks say the same stuff," I said. "'You're witnessing history.' Who cares? I just want some friends."

"Parents!" Valerie honked into a hanky she pulled from her dress pocket.

"Yeah." I waited to see if Valerie would turn her back again. She didn't. "So, if you hate it here so much, and you don't even like white kids, why don't you go back to your old school?"

Valerie sighed so hard her shoulders hiked up to her ears. "Daddy says I have to be an example. That somebody has to go first and it might as well be Lucy and me."

"Is Lucy your sister? Is that the girl you eat with? How does she like it here?"

"Yeah," Valerie said. "She's only a first grader. She doesn't know how much fun school can be."

"Fun?" School?

Valerie slid the cot pillow behind her back. "On rainy days, we danced in the lunchroom at recess."

"We do that here," I reminded her.

"That folk-dancing mess?" Valerie flapped her hand. "I mean *real* dancing, like the monkey and the twist." She smiled, and I knew she was back in her old school, doing the twist.

"Wish we did that," I said. "I wish somebody would step on that old Paul Jones record."

Valerie giggled. "You aren't very good." Her eyes twinkled, winter-sky coldness gone.

"Don't remind me." I giggled, too. A warm, familiar feeling came over me. The feeling of making a new friend. "Hey, who do you like best? Paul or Ringo?" If she said Paul, we would be friends forever.

"Paul or Ringo who?" Valerie frowned.

"You're kidding, right? The Beatles? Everybody knows the Beatles."

Valerie didn't. Her eyes were question marks.

"They're a rock-and-roll band. They were on *The Ed Sullivan Show*?" I kept trying. "They sing 'I Want to Hold Your Hand'?"

"Oh, them!" Valerie shrugged. "They sing okay for white boys, I guess."

Was she kidding? White boys? Jeb and Andy were white boys! "Well, when you danced at your old school, whose records did you bring?"

Valerie hugged her knees. "The Supremes, the Four Tops, the Temptations."

"Gee, I've never heard of any of them."

"Everybody's heard of the Supremes." Valerie sounded real sure of herself. "You know that song 'Where Did Our Love Go'?"

"Oh yeah." Now I remembered. "That was number one last summer in Chicago. But I haven't heard them since I moved down here. Did they make another record?"

"Are you kidding?" It was Valerie's turn to sound surprised. "What radio station do you listen to?"

"Rebel Radio."

"Oh." Valerie smiled and leaned across the space between the cots. "That's a white station. They don't play Negro music. Everybody I know listens to WOKJ."

"I'll give it a try," I said. Something still bugged me, though. "Why don't you tell your daddy you want to go back to your old school?"

Valerie's smile vanished. "Can't disappoint my daddy. I wish somebody else would do the integrating. I just want my friends back."

"Aren't they still your friends? You probably don't see them as much . . ."

"I don't see them at *all*." Valerie bit her lip. "They think I've got the big head, going to a white school. Think I want to *be* white." She sighed. "They say it's dangerous to come over to my house."

"Why? You got alligators in your yard or something?" I tried to make Valerie smile again, but she wasn't in a smiling mood.

"The Klan's been watching our house." She didn't have to say anything more.

"I'm scared of the Klan, too," I said.

Valerie's gray eyes widened. "What would the Klan want with y'all?"

"My daddy is an FBI agent."

"Oh." Valerie smiled sadly. "What did the Klan do to y'all?"

"Nasty phone calls mostly, telling us to go back to Chicago."

"Shoot, that's nothing. They put sugar in our gas tank. Dead rats in the mailbox. We gave our dog away 'cause Daddy was afraid the Klan would kill her." Valerie ticked off these things as if they were nothing. I knew they weren't.

"I'm scared someone will shoot through my window," I said. "My bed is right under it. I sleep hanging off the edge so I can hit the floor and roll under the bed if I have to."

"I sleep *on* the floor. Saves time, just in case." Valerie's eyes met mine. She *understood.* Understood like no one else in the sixth grade ever could.

"Want to be friends?" I blurted.

Valerie looked away. "I told you. Just 'cause I go to school here don't mean I have to be friends with y'all." She laughed, but not like anything was funny. "You gonna invite me over to your house after school?" The warm, easy feeling disappeared.

"Well, uh . . ." I hadn't thought that far ahead.

"Or you gonna come home with me?" She pointed to herself. Her fingernails were bitten down past the quick. Little blood crusts circled the thumbnails. It hurt just to look at them.

Mrs. Messer poked her head in the door. "If y'all feel good enough to talk, y'all can go back to class," she said. "Put your shoes on and scoot."

Valerie slid into her loafers, brushed the wrinkles out of her skirt, and glided out the clinic door. She never looked back.

I thought about Valerie the rest of the afternoon. I never thought somebody wouldn't be my friend because I was *white*.

I thought myself into one big, fat headache.

My head still hurt when Mama picked me up after school for an appointment with Dr. Warren.

"Don't even think about it," said Mama as I reached for the radio knob. "That music makes me nuts. Driving in rain is bad enough. Why don't you try talking to your old mother for a change?" She grinned. For a moment she was her old Chicago self. Maybe she could help make sense of things.

"Mama, are Negroes really different from white people?"

"Of course not!" Mama frowned, but didn't take her eyes off the road.

"Jeb says they are. Everybody in my class says they are."

"Well," Mama said, "what do you think?"

"Me?" I watched the windshield wipers tick back and forth. "I don't think so. I talked to Valerie Taylor today. She didn't seem all that different to me. Except she barely knew who the Beatles are."

It seemed so simple when you thought of it that way. Except that I knew it *wasn't* that simple.

"Is that so?" Old Mama had vanished. And this Mama wasn't listening. "Keep an eye peeled for a parking place."

There weren't any.

"You'd think a doctor would have his own parking lot," Mama griped. "I'll drop you off while I keep looking."

Dr. Warren's office looked pretty much like every other doctor's office. Hard plastic chairs, fluorescent lights that hummed and flickered, boring magazines. I knew by now to bring something to read. I flipped open *16 Magazine* to "Will Jane and Paul Get Married?"

I squirmed in my seat, trying to concentrate on the article. I needed a bathroom. Now.

Dr. Warren's crabby nurse walked by with a stack of files.

"Excuse me, but where's the rest room?" I whispered.

"Bathroom's down the hall at the end," she called as she disappeared behind the reception desk.

Thanks for letting everyone know.

There were three doors at the end of the hall. I opened the closest one and fumbled for the light switch.

I blinked. The light *was* on, a single dim ceiling bulb.

I was not alone.

Negroes on backless benches or the floor, slumped against the walls, filled the windowless room.

"I was looking for the bathroom," I said to no one in particular.

What are these people doing back here?

A young man with a mustache and bloodshot eyes snorted and looked away. A motherly looking woman said, "Child, you ought not to be here."

"Why not? What is this place?"

"We're waitin' to see the doctor," said the woman in a soft voice.

I had never seen a Negro patient at Dr. Warren's. "It's so dark back here. Why don't you sit out front?"

The woman shook her head. "You ain't from round here, are

you? No, we sits back here. When all the white folks is taken care of, then they come for us."

"You stupid girl, not *that* door." The crabby nurse swooped in front of me and slammed the door. She pulled a key from her pocket and locked the door with a sharp twist. "Callie," she hollered over her shoulder. "Who left the colored waiting room open? It's supposed to stay locked!"

Colored waiting room? A *locked* waiting room?

Then I got it. Really got it.

There was no way for a Negro girl and a white girl in Mississippi to be friends. No way.

6

JACKSON DAILY JOURNAL, Friday, October 23, 1964

FBI INVESTIGATES BOMBING OF NEGRO HOUSE
Owners Suspected of Civil Rights Activities

★"What are you going to be for Halloween?" I asked Jeb at the bus stop one morning.

"Halloween? That's for little kids." Jeb shifted a peppermint toothpick from cheek to cheek. "It's football season," he said, like that was *the* answer.

It figured. Down South, everybody was football crazy. The boys collected football cards and talked about professional players like they lived next door. Everybody had a favorite college or high-school team. And of course, there were the Cheerleaders.

I perched on an empty bike rack and watched them practice on the playground. They practiced every morning, but today was different. Today they wore cheerleading uniforms.

Dip, stomp, clap, and twirl. Their red skirts swirled out in perfect circles, matching shorts showing beneath. The girls jumped, their legs crooked sideways, hair flying in the crisp breeze. For a heartbeat, I was one of them, leaping, happy and free in the autumn air.

For the first time, cheerleading didn't seem silly. That sassy, switching skirt could make me a whole different person. A girl with straight hair, flipped at the ends. A girl with lots of friends who would never call her "Yankee Girl."

The morning sun glinted off Carrie's red hair and shiny braces. Then it hit me. I needed to *become* a Cheerleader. Why hadn't I thought of that before?

I wanted friends. I wanted a jumper with a swirly skirt. I *would* be a Cheerleader. I'd ask Mary Martha about it. At least *she* talked to me. Sometimes.

The first bell clanged. Kids jumped from the swings and jungle gym and lined up. Miss LeFleur stood at the front door, ready to drop the record-player arm on the "King Cotton March." We filed in to the same record every morning.

"Mark time, march. Left, right, left, right." Miss LeFleur smiled and pumped her arms as her polished penny loafers kept time. Today she wore a pink sweater and a gray pleated skirt. Miss Gruen wore brown every single day. I bet even her underwear was brown.

"Mary Martha." I tapped her shoulder. "How did you get to be a cheerleader?"

"My mama made me." She sighed. "Saranne's mama's in charge and she asked my mama if I wanted to do it. I didn't, but Mama said I had to."

"Sixth grade, forward," Miss LeFleur sang out.

Mary Martha and I stomped up the steps and down the hall to 6B.

"All you need is a uniform," she said. "Mama has the jumper pattern. We all used the same one."

"That's all?" Becoming a Cheerleader couldn't be *this* easy.

Mary Martha shrugged. "Sure. It's YMCA cheerleaders and anyone who wants to can be one. As long as they belong to the Y."

"We do. But what about the cheers?"

"What about them?" Mary Martha smiled. "Do they look hard to you?"

"Then why are you guys always practicing?"

"Because Saranne makes a big deal out of everything. I'll tell them at recess you want to join. And I'll bring the pattern Monday."

I was going to be a Cheerleader. Happiness hummed inside me. Soon I'd have friends to share my jokes and secrets and Beatles records with.

Then Mary Martha told the Cheerleaders at recess.

Saranne balled her fists on her hips and glared. "You're not in charge, Mary Martha Goode. You think just anybody can be a cheerleader? Next thing, old Valerie'll want to be a cheerleader."

The humming feeling sputtered and died.

"Anybody *can* be a cheerleader," Mary Martha pointed out. "As long as they belong to the Y."

"I ain't cheering with no nigra." Debbie pouted as she unwrapped a stick of lime Fruit Stripe. "My mama wouldn't like it."

Mary Martha blew her bangs out of her eyes. "Valerie doesn't want to be a cheerleader. But Alice does."

Debbie smacked her gum. Saranne folded her arms across her flat chest and scowled. Carrie yawned. Cheryl picked at her cuticles.

Nobody looked at me.

"So that's that," said Mary Martha.

I was a Cheerleader.

Not that I noticed any big change on the bus that afternoon. I sat with a third grader, right in front of the Cheerleaders. They sat in their usual backseat, singing "Can't Buy Me Love" to Debbie's transistor.

Still Invisible Alice.

I turned around. "Saranne?"

She looked up from the *Song Hits* magazine she and Debbie shared. "Yeah? Whaddya want, Yankee Girl?"

"When's the next football game?"

"Next Saturday."

"Where?"

"I'll write you some directions," said Saranne. "It's kinda complicated."

That was nice of her. The happy humming cranked back to life.

The bus screeched to a stop at my corner. I started to stand, but couldn't. I was stuck. I peeled myself off the fake leather. Something dangled down the back of my leg.

Gum. Bright-pink bubble gum plastered to my skirt and the seat, with big strands stringing in between.

"Hey, Yankee Girl. You got gum on your skirt," snickered Debbie. "You oughta look before you sit." The Cheerleaders burst into nose-snorting laughter.

I stomped off the bus, everyone whooping and pointing at my gummy behind. I wished they'd all drop dead.

By Sunday night I wasn't mad anymore. Maybe the Cheerleaders hadn't done it. Maybe they laughed because it was funny. If it had happened to somebody else, I would've thought it was funny, too.

I still wanted to be a Cheerleader.

Mary Martha waited for me on the playground Monday morning.

"I've got the uniform pattern." She handed me a split-sided manila envelope with a crumpled tissue-paper pattern crammed inside.

"Isn't there supposed to be a picture on the envelope?" I asked.

"Carrie's baby brother peed on the real envelope and it was too nasty to keep," explained Mary Martha. "Can your mama make it by Friday? We're wearing our uniforms to school on Friday again."

"Sure." I wasn't at all sure. How many times had Mama said, "I really don't like to sew"?

Mama frowned at the pattern pieces spread across the kitchen table that afternoon.

"I don't know about this," she said. "I really don't like to sew. There isn't even a picture to go by. Looks like the bib piece is missing. I need a new pattern. Let's go to the store."

The fabric-store clerk examined the wrinkled wad of pattern pieces.

"This is pattern number 7602," she said, peering through her bifocals.

"Fine," said Mama. "Where is pattern 7602?"

"Discontinued." The clerk handed the pieces back. "This pattern is at least ten years old."

Mama and the clerk spread the pieces across the cutting counter and figured how much fabric we needed. While they did that, I checked out the red cloth.

I didn't know there were that many kinds of red! Brick red, tomato red, fire-engine red. The clerk yanked out bolt after bolt of red, red, and more red, unrolling them across the cutting counter. I tried to remember exactly what color the jumpers were.

"*Pick* one," said Mama, her voice one step from losing her temper.

"Okay, this one." I pointed to the fire-engine red. The clerk slashed off a length of material and folded it into a bag before I could change my mind. I hoped it was the right color.

Mama hadn't told me the whole truth. She didn't dislike sewing; she *hated* sewing.

I stood for hours while she pinned pattern pieces to my clothes.

"Hold still." Mama jerked a tissue-paper strap. A pin rammed my shoulder.

"Ow!"

"Told you to hold still," muttered Mama. "This would go faster if you'd stop wiggling and cooperate." She tugged on the bib piece she'd cut from newspaper. A pin jabbed, I jumped, and the newspaper bib tore in Mama's hand. We started over, pinning and tugging.

"When will it be finished?" I asked.

"Don't pester, Alice." Mama rubbed her nose where her sewing glasses pinched.

"Is it too much to expect a hot meal at the end of the day?" Daddy griped as we sat down to tuna fish sandwiches and potato chips for the third night in a row. This *would* be the one week he was home for dinner every night.

"It is if you're trying to sew from a pattern with half the pieces and instructions missing," snapped Mama.

Far into the night I heard the sewing machine race down lengths of red cotton. Well, not exactly race. More like start and stop. Then mumbling, and I knew that the thread had run out or the needle had broken.

By Thursday night, we were down to peanut butter sandwiches, no potato chips, and no Mama. From the guest room, I heard the sewing machine start and stop. Start and stop. Dinner was over, my homework done, and I had rolled my hair on orange-juice cans when Mama opened my bedroom door.

"It's finished." She leaned against the door frame. Her hair was mussed, there were dark circles under her eyes, but she smiled. "Come see."

I tore down the hall to the guest room. Draped across the bed was my uniform! The white felt "P" for Parnell stood out, bright and bold against the red bib. I saw myself twirling and jumping, the skirt a perfect circle around me.

I could hardly wait for tomorrow.

7

FBI JAIL FOUR IN ASSAULT
ON CIVIL RIGHTS WORKERS

★Friday. Spirit Day. The first day of My Life as a Cheerleader.

I yanked the orange-juice cans out of my hair in front of the bathroom mirror. I looked like Jane Asher. Almost.

I started to get dressed. Then I realized that Mama hadn't made the blouse that went under the uniform jumper. Or the matching shorts.

"Just keep your skirt down," said Mama. "And you have white blouses."

But not one with short sleeves. I found a white blouse in my closet and rolled up the long sleeves.

I checked myself in the big mirror in Mama and Daddy's room. Something about the jumper wasn't right. But what?

Mama watched from the open door. "There wasn't enough material to make the skirt as full as the pattern called for. I didn't think it would matter."

But it did.

I twirled. No swirl. No magic.

The blouse sleeves unrolled. My bangs frizzed. The bib gapped like a kangaroo pouch. The white felt "P" doubled over to look like a "D."

"I knew that made-up bib pattern wasn't right," said Mama.

"It's all right, Mama." But it wasn't.

I wanted to tell Mama that this was the most perfect cheerleading uniform in the world. I knew she wanted to tell me that I looked perfect in it.

But we couldn't. It wasn't the truth. So we just pretended instead.

I trudged off to the bus stop.

"Holy moly!" Jeb almost swallowed his toothpick. "Are you supposed to be a cheerleader or something? Halloween ain't till tomorrow, you know."

"Of course she's a cheerleader," said Pammie, although she didn't sound too sure herself. She straightened my blouse collar, stepped back, and squinted.

"You need lip gloss." She dug a tiny compact out of her purse. She stuck a finger in something that looked like Vaseline and smeared it on my mouth.

I ran my tongue across my lips. It tasted like waxy strawberries.

"Don't do that," Pammie said. "You're licking it off."

"How do I look?"

"Better," Pammie said, but not like she meant it. She handed me her pocket mirror. My lips looked greasy, my hair like unraveled yarn. Same old Yankee Girl.

The bus pulled up and the door wheezed open. From the back, Saranne yelled, "Hey, Yankee Girl, sit here. Shove over, Debbie. Let Yankee Girl sit down."

Oh, well. It would take them a while to get used to calling me Alice. At least I wasn't invisible.

I wedged in next to Debbie.

"Hey," Debbie protested. "You're squishing me." She gave me a hip butt, sending my rear out in the aisle. I didn't care. I was sitting with the Cheerleaders!

Debbie flounced and smoothed her skirt beneath her. Then I noticed.

My skirt was fire-engine red. Debbie's was tomato red. So were Saranne's and Carrie's and Cheryl's.

I had picked the wrong color material.

"Hey, your uniform is . . ." Debbie began.

"Perfect, just perfect," Saranne jumped in.

"Really?" It didn't look perfect to me.

"Looks fine. Doesn't it look fine, Carrie?" Saranne nudged Carrie.

"Sure," said Carrie, as if she couldn't care less.

Invisible Alice was back.

Mary Martha waited for us on the playground.

"Doesn't Yankee Girl's jumper look fab?" Saranne said in a peppy voice.

Mary Martha shot her an odd look. "Well, it's . . ."

"Fine," Debbie interrupted.

"I suppose it's okay." Mary Martha looked me up and down. "Tell your mother if she moves the buttons on the straps, your bib won't droop so much."

"Okay. Thanks." Everyone just stood around, looking at each other. "Aren't you all going to practice?" I'd stopped saying "you guys," but hadn't gotten the hang of saying "y'all."

"Nah, we're all practiced out," said Saranne. "Don't worry. You'll do fine."

Did I imagine it, or did she wink at Cheryl? Did Cheryl wink back?

"Well, then, where's the game?" I asked.

"I have the directions all written down for you." Saranne took a folded sheet of notebook paper from her purse.

"Couldn't I just ride with you?"

"Gee, sorry," Saranne said. "Our car only has room for five."

I could sit on someone's lap.

But I didn't want to sound pushy.

There was only one person left.

"Are you crazy?" sputtered Jeb. "Me? Bring a girl to a game? And don't go asking Pammie or Mama either. You do and we won't be friends no more."

So I was stuck with Mama.

"Saranne certainly gives detailed directions," she commented as she studied Saranne's tiny cursive. "We shouldn't have any trouble finding this." Just to make sure though, we left the house a whole hour before game time.

A good thing, too. Half an hour later, we found ourselves in the middle of a Negro neighborhood. We pulled into a Texaco station to get our bearings.

"Maybe we made a wrong turn somewhere." Mama took off her sunglasses and peered at Saranne's directions.

We must have. We were in a whole other world. A Negro world. Men wiping windshields at the Texaco. Women dragging two-wheeled wire carts of groceries. Boys and girls speeding by on bikes and skates. All Negroes.

"Twist and Shout" blared from a radio on a kitchen chair outside the gas station. But not the Beatles' version.

"That was the Isley Brothers, here on WOKJ," oozed a smooth-talking deejay.

Mothers scolded kids for biking on the sidewalk. The gas-station men argued about the World Series. Boys and girls shouted teasing insults at each other. If I closed my eyes, I could pretend I was in my own neighborhood.

But I wasn't. We didn't belong here.

A man in a Texaco shirt came up to Mama's open window. "Luther" was embroidered in red across his shirt pocket.

"Are you lost, ma'am?" Luther said. He didn't look at her, I noticed.

"I think so," said Mama. "We're looking for Dilworth Field."

Luther couldn't have looked more surprised if she'd said we were looking for President Johnson.

"Yes, ma'am. You in the right place. You sure y'all are looking for Dilworth?"

"If that's where they're playing sixth-grade football."

Luther looked doubtful. "Well, if you're sure. Go down two blocks and Dilworth's on the right. Football field directly behind. Can't miss it."

Mama nosed the Chrysler back into the street. Two blocks down, I spied a sign.

"Look. Dilworth High School."

Mama swung into a patch of dirt and dead grass that was the parking lot. People streamed past us, heading for the field. Moms and dads with lawn chairs. Kids in hooded sweatshirts. Boys in football pants and jerseys, swinging helmets by the chin strap. Cheerleaders in jumpers like mine except different colors: green, purple, and orange.

All Negroes.

"Think I'll walk down with you," said Mama.

"Okay, if you want to," I said, casual-like. I didn't feel casual. I felt like the whitest white person alive.

We walked across the rutted parking lot, pretending not to notice the looks thrown our way. Where were Jeb and the football players? Saranne and the Cheerleaders?

We rounded the corner of the school and could finally see the field. I picked out the two teams and their cheerleaders. One set dressed in green, one in purple.

Both Negro.

"Maybe everybody's late. Maybe Saranne got it wrong," I babbled. Panic knotted my stomach.

"Something's not right here." Mama's new wrinkle deepened. "I'm getting to the bottom of this."

"Mama, don't." I knew she'd do something terribly embarrassing.

She marched over to a group of mothers in the end zone. The mothers looked pretty much like mine: capri pants and sweaters, headscarves and rainbow-colored Keds. Except they were Negro.

"Excuse me, but when does Parnell School play?" Mama asked a woman in a pink headscarf.

The woman looked at Mama as if she were a Martian.

"Y'all ever heard of a Parnell School?" Headscarf Woman asked the other mothers. To Mama, "This game is between Brown and Miller."

I had never heard of Brown or Miller.

The women whispered among themselves.

Headscarf Woman looked at Mama and shook her head. "Is this Parnell a white school?"

"Not anymore," said Mama. "Alice, what is the name of that Negro girl in your class?"

"Valerie Taylor." What did Valerie have to do with anything?

The Negro women perked up.

"Reverend Taylor's girl?" said Headscarf Woman.

Mama nodded.

"Ma'am, Valerie Taylor goes to a white school. White schools don't play down here." The woman's eyes looked sad but kind. "Somebody's playing a joke on you."

It all made sense now. The jumper pattern that didn't come together, the cheers no one wanted me to learn, Saranne's directions. The gum on my skirt. The Y said they had to let me be a cheerleader . . . but the Cheerleaders didn't have to let me cheer.

I didn't look at Mama. I didn't want to see her horribly sympathetic look.

The purple and green uniforms and the brown faces blurred with the tears I held inside.

Valerie was wrong. I knew how it felt to be the only one. The only one.

8

FIRE WRECKS CHURCH USED
FOR CIVIL RIGHTS ACTIVITIES

★"I've a mind to call that Saranne's mother," said Mama as she gunned the car out of the Dilworth parking lot. "Sending us on a wild-goose chase like that."

"No," I said, louder than I needed to. "I mean, this is between me and Saranne." I slumped down in the car seat, folded my arms against my chest, and hoped that Mama wouldn't say anything more.

I should've known better.

"Well, then sit up and snap out of it, young lady." Mama sounded crabby. Maybe because I wouldn't let her talk to Mrs. Russell. Or maybe because she had done all that sewing on my uniform for nothing. I tried to explain.

"See, I think the Cheerleaders were all in on it. Not just Saranne." This was harder than I thought it would be.

"Why on earth would your new friends do such a thing?"

"Because I'm a Yankee." There. I said it. Would Mama understand?

Mama frowned. "Then just think how much worse the Negroes have it. Stop feeling sorry for yourself. Someday you'll be glad you lived in 1964. You can tell your children about it."

"Who cares?" I stared out the windshield at nothing. So much for talking to Mama. Hadn't she ever been eleven? Didn't she remember what it was like? I guessed not.

I spent the weekend hiding in my room, wishing I were dead. I just knew the whole sixth grade was laughing about the Cheerleaders' little joke.

"Hey, girl," said Jeb at the bus stop Monday morning. "Where was you Saturday?"

So the Cheerleaders hadn't told *everybody*.

"We got lost," I said. "Which wouldn't have happened if I'd gone with you." It was sort of the truth.

"Sorry." He gave me a crooked Paul McCartney smile. "You can go with me next time."

"There isn't a next time," I snapped. "That was the last game." Something else the Cheerleaders hadn't bothered to tell me. Mama had called the Y to ask for the rest of the football schedule. There was no rest of the schedule.

Jeb shrugged. "I owe you one, okay?"

"You bet you owe me," I said. "I'm holding you to that."

Jeb grinned and poked a finger in my elbow. "Or?"

"Or I'll tell your mama you wouldn't let me ride with you."

Jeb stopped grinning. "Okay, okay." The look in his eyes made me feel powerful.

Until we got to school. Jeb wandered off with Andy and Skipper. I leaned against the oak tree and watched the Cheerleaders trade Beatles cards. Last Friday, I thought I'd stand with them forever. Last Friday, a million years ago.

"Alice, I heard what happened Saturday. I'm sorry."

I turned to see Mary Martha, looking serious.

"S'okay," I mumbled.

"No, it's not," she said. "White people in a colored neighborhood? Who knows what could've happened?" She looked me in the eye. "I just want you to know that I didn't have anything to do with it."

"You didn't?" I figured the whole sixth grade had been in on the joke.

"I most certainly did not," she huffed. "C'mon. I'll prove it to you." She dragged me over to where the Cheerleaders huddled at the edge of the playground.

"Saranne, did I know about what y'all pulled on Alice?" Mary Martha demanded.

Saranne kicked the crumbling playground asphalt with the toe of her loafer. "No, we didn't tell Mary Martha." She smiled, her pointy teeth winking at me. "We didn't mean anything by it."

It wasn't a great apology, but it would do.

From then on, I stood with the Cheerleaders before school. Not in the center, but not at the edges either. Kind of halfway in the middle.

Nobody but Mary Martha ever talked to me. She wasn't exactly friendly. More like polite. After being invisible, polite felt like friendly. I didn't care. I belonged. Sort of.

"So that misunderstanding with the cheerleaders is cleared up?" Mama asked at supper that night.

"Hmmm," I answered with a mouthful of peas. I hoped she'd tell me not to talk with my mouth full and drop the subject.

"How is Valerie getting along?" asked Daddy.

I swallowed the peas. "Okay, I guess." She wasn't, but it was too complicated to explain. Debbie threw Valerie's sweater in the trash can again. Carrie smeared paste on Valerie's chair while she was at the pencil sharpener. Cheryl left ugly notes in Valerie's cubby.

Saranne had pulled the worst trick of all. She'd sprinkled skunk oil inside Valerie's desk. It smelled like a million dead, rotting skunks.

"You better hope that bottle doesn't come open in your purse," said Carrie.

It didn't. But the trick backfired because the whole class had to breathe that eye-watering stink. Everyone blamed Valerie. After all, it was her desk.

"Told you niggers stink," Leland said about a thousand times.

Miss Gruen banged open all the windows even though it was freezing outside. The janitor washed the room down with Lysol, which did *not* get rid of the smell. Now 6B smelled like skunk *and* Lysol. The odor hung on for days.

Through it all, Valerie never cried, never lost her temper.

One chilly November morning Mary Martha was absent. I

didn't know what else to do, so I stood with the Cheerleaders as usual.

As we huddled against the cold, Saranne said, "I'm getting tired of doing the same old stuff to Valerie Coon. Hey, Yankee Girl. You got any ideas?"

"Who, me?" Saranne? Talking to me?

"Forget her," said Cheryl. "Yankees like nigras."

"My daddy says all Yankees are nigger lovers," said Debbie. "He says they even marry them and have half-nigger kids." She unwrapped a stick of lime Fruit Stripe, popped it in her mouth, then popped it out again. "Bleah." She pulled at a long strand of hair. "I hate it when I get hair in my mouth. 'Specially when I'm chewing gum."

"Gross," said Carrie. "Stick that gum back in your mouth."

"Nooo." Debbie stared at the wet wad of green in her palm. "Let's stick it in her hair."

"Whose hair?" Carrie blinked, looking confused.

"Coon Girl's hair," said Debbie. "Let's stick gum in her hair. She'll have to shave her head to get it out." She grinned. A big evil grin.

The Cheerleaders' eyes lit up with a nasty glimmer.

"Fab," said Cheryl.

"Valerie has that ponytail . . ." began Carrie.

"And we could stick it right at the top of . . ." Saranne went on.

"It'll never come out. She'll look a mess," interrupted Debbie.

My stomach roller-coastered into my shoes. They wouldn't *really* do that, would they?

This was worse than hiding Valerie's sweater or sprinkling skunk oil. The sweater always turned up. Room 6B stopped stinking. This was permanent. Or permanent for as long as it took for hair to grow out.

Of all the mean, nasty schemes the Cheerleaders had cooked up, this one was the worst. I hoped they would forget about it by recess.

They didn't forget.

"Alice," called Saranne as we lined up for volleyball. "We're meeting at my house after school to talk about you-know-what." She rubbed her hands together in a businesslike way. "You'll be there." She wasn't asking me.

"I'll be there."

I was thrilled to be included. None of the Cheerleaders had invited me over to their house so far.

Then I thought about what I was being invited over for. I decided to go anyway. After all, I didn't have to do anything. Just be there. Besides, I didn't want to make Saranne mad.

We all crammed into Saranne's bedroom. It was hot with the furnace vents blasting and all of us jammed together on Saranne's canopy bed. Hot, and very pink. Bubble-gum pink. Pink walls, pink bedspread, pink shag rug.

The bubble-gum-colored walls swirled around me.

I should go home. I should go home and never talk to any of these girls again.

I thought about how good it felt to belong.

I stayed.

Saranne's plan was so stupid it was brilliant. The Cheerleaders would rush Valerie and knock her down, like it was an accident. During the confusion, Cheryl would plant the wad of gum in Valerie's hair.

"You really think this is gonna work?" I asked.

"Of course it'll work." Saranne sounded confident. "We'll do it tomorrow at recess."

I thought it over as I rode Blue Rover home through the damp dusk. It felt good being in on such a big secret.

It felt really crummy, too. In Chicago, I would've said, "Hey, what's Valerie ever done to you?" But this wasn't Chicago. Here I was just Yankee Girl. Who would listen to me?

The next morning, I wobbled off the bus feeling queasy. It was a beautiful blue-sky day. Too beautiful for mean tricks. Maybe Valerie would be absent.

Nope. Right on time, the Taylors' white Chevy station wagon pulled up to the curb. Out jumped Valerie. Did her ponytail look longer and shinier than usual?

"Look at that." Saranne sounded disgusted. "She's wearing a hair bow right where the gum is supposed to go."

"So the plan is off?" I hoped.

"Of course not!" Saranne snapped. "We'll stick it *below* the bow."

All morning I hoped something would happen. The office would forget to ring the recess bell. A Russian missile would fall on the playground. Time would stand still.

Time didn't stand still, the Russians weren't mad at Americans that week, and the recess bell rang right on time.

"Hurry up," whispered Carrie, flinging her coat over her

head. She grabbed me by the wrist and threw me into line ahead of her. Saranne squeezed ahead of Valerie, glanced over her shoulder, and winked at me.

Carrie nudged something small into my palm. Two pieces of Dubble Bubble gum.

Put it in your pocket. They can't do this without gum.

Ahead of me, Cheryl glanced over her shoulder. "Where's the gum, Yankee Girl?" she whispered loudly.

It's not even my gum. Maybe she'll just chew it.

I passed her the gum.

We filed past the fifth-, fourth-, third-grade rooms. Closer, closer to the playground doors. The library. The water fountain. Second grade, first grade. Then out the double doors to the playground and into the bright blue morning.

Saranne stopped short to pull up her kneesocks. Valerie plowed right into her.

"Hey, why don't you watch where you're going?" Saranne yelled at Valerie.

"Yeah, wake up," Carrie chimed in. She gave Saranne a hand while pushing Valerie down. Cheryl tripped and landed on the heap with Debbie right behind her. I just stood there watching the five-headed girl-monster struggling on the asphalt playground, a tangle of elbows and knees and waving hands. A loafer flew in the air, bopping Leland in the nose.

"Ow!" he howled. "Creepy girls!"

The monster flopped around for what seemed like forever. Then, one by one, the Cheerleaders got up. When Cheryl stepped away, a wet wad of sticky pink gum blossomed just below Valerie's hair bow. Last of all, Valerie struggled to her feet, brushing herself off.

The rest of the class jostled closer for a better look.

Oh no. What have I done?

Hey, you *didn't do anything. It was Debbie's idea.*

Miss Gruen burst out the double doors. "What happened here?"

"Nothing, ma'am." Valerie swiped asphalt crumbs off her knees.

"Looks like plenty happened." Miss Gruen pinched Valerie's ponytail between her fingers and peered through her glasses. "Why, this looks like gum."

"Ma'am?" Valerie's voice trembled.

"You have a sizable wad of chewing gum in your hair. Bubble gum, to be precise." Miss Gruen pulled a hanky from her pocket, wiped her fingers, then blasted her whistle.

All of 6B came running.

"There is gum in Valerie's hair," Miss Gruen said to the class. "It didn't grow there. Can anyone tell me what happened?"

We looked at each other, then away. A few giggled. Leland's wide grin said he wished he'd thought of it first.

"Saranne stopped to pull up her socks and everybody fell on top of her," Jeb volunteered.

"Who is 'everybody'?" demanded Miss Gruen.

"Debbie and Carrie was all I could see," said Jeb.

"Debbie, did you have gum in your mouth?" demanded Miss Gruen.

"No, ma'am," said Debbie, grinning. "I *still* have gum in my mouth." She blew a big bubble to prove it. Miss Gruen pointed to the trash can, then turned to Carrie.

"I don't chew gum," Carrie said before she was asked. "I have braces. See?" She pulled the sides of her mouth wide so Miss Gruen could see.

"That will do, Carrie," said Toad Woman. "I'll tend to this matter later."

Valerie stood next to Miss Gruen. Tears slid down her freckled cheeks.

My stomach hurt.

Miss Gruen sighed. "Let's go to the office and see what we can do about this. The rest of you, back to class."

"Hey, what happened to recess?" protested Leland.

"Recess is over," said Miss Gruen as she and Valerie disappeared into the building. The rest of us followed, dragging our feet all the way to 6B.

Miss Gruen was back in five minutes. With Mr. Thibodeaux.

"We tried peanut butter, but it didn't work." Miss Gruen glared at us. "Now she has peanut butter *and* gum in her hair. She'll have to have the gum cut out."

A girl giggled in the back of the room. Leland laughed out loud.

"This isn't funny, boys and girls," said Mr. Thibodeaux. "Why, this might even be on the news tonight."

Mr. Thibodeaux talked on and on about being good citizens and loving thy neighbor, but I wasn't listening. On the news!

Walter Cronkite sticking a microphone in my face. "Alice Ann Moxley, did you know about this plan? And why didn't you stop them?"

I couldn't sleep that night. Behind closed eyelids I saw the tears on Valerie's cheeks. Her trembling lip. The pink rose of gum in her hair.

After a lot of flopping and flipping, I finally fell asleep. What woke me? Car doors slamming? Laughter? Or was it the odd smell that drifted through the half-open window. A smell that reminded me of summer and lawn mowers.

Gasoline. Gasoline?

Something bright flashed behind my closed eyelids. Lightning?

Rubbing my eyes, I looked out my bedroom window. It swam into focus. The letters "KKK." On fire. In the grass. In our front yard.

9

WHITE CITIZENS' COUNCIL
DECRIES RACE MIXING

★The police poked around the scorched grass. "Bunch of kids horsing around," they decided.

"Horsing around, my foot," said Mama, tight-lipped.

Kids or the Klan? Daddy discouraged both by hanging floodlights at the corners of the house. They glared in my eyes at night. Not that I slept much anyway. Life was just too crazy. It flip-flopped between normal and weird.

School was the normal part. I got a C in math. In folk dancing, we moved on to the "Mexican Serape Dance." Miss Gruen looked more like a toad every day.

Then I'd go home, the weird part. "KKK" branded in our yard. People on the phone telling us to "go back to Yankee-land." Sometimes they used dirty words. After a while, weird seemed normal. I guess you can get used to anything. Like being scared all the time.

Valerie returned to school with her hair cut off. Cropped to her scalp, the new hairdo showed off the shape of her head and made her eyes look bigger.

"Nigger gal looks like a nigger boy now," Leland sneered.

"Well, she sure looks different." Saranne sounded disappointed that Valerie didn't look perfectly hideous.

I was all mixed up about Valerie. I felt crummy about how the Cheerleaders treated her. But hanging out with the Cheerleaders felt good. Sort of. They still weren't all that friendly to me. I wanted friendly.

Like that day in the clinic with Valerie.

I gave friendship with Valerie one more chance.

"I like your hair." We were alone in the rest room. I lathered my hands. Valerie stood at the next sink, doing the same.

"Thank you." She kept her eyes on her soapy hands.

"What do you call it? A crew cut?"

Valerie's eyes narrowed. Did she think I was making fun of her?

"It's called a natural. African women wear their hair this way." She dried her hands on a brown paper towel, folded it neatly in quarters, and tossed it in the trash. "I told you I don't need white friends."

Fine! If she didn't want to be friends, I didn't either. I had the Cheerleaders.

And I had more important things to think about. Like Christmas.

———

The Christmas season officially started the day after Thanksgiving vacation. The whole school smelled and sounded different. Instead of the old-lunch-and-Lysol smell, the halls shimmered with the aroma of fir tree, rubber cement, and gold spray paint. In front of the office stood a fir tree. Bit by bit, the tree acquired paste-smeared paper chains, cockeyed Dixie-cup angels, and glitter-covered Styrofoam balls.

The halls echoed with classes practicing for the Christmas pageant: the fifth grade singing "God Rest Ye Merry Gentlemen" or the first grade screaming "Jingle Bells" at the top of their little lungs.

"Same old pageant," Jeb griped. "Each grade does the same skit every year."

"What does the sixth grade do?"

Jeb frowned. "The manger thing. Shepherds, angels, the whole bit."

"Sounds okay to me. Why the frown?"

"At church, I always get stuck being a Wise Man." Jeb kicked a rock into the storm sewer. "Wear my dad's bathrobe with cotton stuck to my chin? In front of the whole school and their parents? No, thanks."

"I wouldn't mind being Mary," I said.

"You might could be. The teachers assign parts, except for the angel. You have to try out for that. The angel sings a solo."

That counted me out. I couldn't carry a tune with both hands. But at lunch the next day, I discovered I was the only sixth-grade girl not trying out. Or at least the only one besides Valerie.

"I want to be the angel." Saranne sipped her milk, and waited for someone to say, "Of course you'll be the angel, Saranne."

Nobody did.

"So do I," said Debbie.

"I can sing better'n you," huffed Saranne.

"Yeah, but I look like an angel." Debbie batted her eyelashes. She *was* the prettiest cheerleader. And boy, did she know it!

Tryouts were during recess. We squirmed on the splintery auditorium seats as girl after girl sang "The First Noel," with Miss Gruen at the piano. Some were pretty good; some were just plain terrible.

Saranne glided onstage, very sure of herself. Then she opened her mouth.

Jeb covered his ears. "Sounds like a cat caught in a lawn mower."

Saranne smiled her wolf-fang smile and waited for everyone to tell her how great she was.

Nobody did.

Debbie's turn. She swished her behind all the way up to the stage.

"She just thinks she's it." Saranne poked out her lower lip.

"Sssh," said Andy. "I want to hear her sing."

Debbie sang sort of twangy, but on key.

"She sounds like that country singer that died. Patsy Cline?" said Jeb.

"I think she sounds good," said Andy, jaw jutting.

Debbie prissed off the stage, looking very pleased with herself.

"Valerie Taylor," called Miss LeFleur.

Valerie? Whispers rippled through the auditorium.

"Told you she was uppity," Debbie said. "She don't know her place."

"This oughta be good." Leland reared back in his seat, one knee hiked over the other, arms folded against his plaid shirt.

Valerie made her way down the aisle, her pleated skirt dipping behind her knees as she climbed the stage steps. She stood by the piano, hands clasped, took a deep breath, and fixed her eyes on the back of the room. And sang.

She sang like a grown woman, her voice warm and sweet. Like molasses and honey mixed up together. She sang the whole song without a quiver or a giggle.

"Wow," whispered Jeb as Valerie returned to her seat. "Holy wow."

"She's got it," said Mary Martha. "Nobody else was even half as good."

"Well, a nigra can't be the angel," Saranne said in a sure voice.

"Why not?" Mary Martha asked.

Saranne blew her bangs out of her eyes. "Have you ever seen a picture of a nigra angel?"

"Have you ever seen a *real* angel?" Mary Martha shot back.

"I don't know what y'all are fussing about," said Andy. "Debbie's gonna get it."

Onstage, Miss Gruen and Miss LeFleur sat at the piano, heads bent over a clipboard.

"You just like Debbie," said Jeb. "I bet she's your girlfriend."

"Is not," said Andy. "You take that back." He balled up his fist. So did Jeb.

Miss Gruen crashed a chord on the piano, and the boys dropped their fists.

"Attention, please." Miss Gruen stepped to center stage, clipboard in hand. "Remember, your behavior during practice will be reflected in your conduct grade." She gave Andy and Jeb the Look. "The following students will have roles in the Christmas program. Everyone else will sing in the chorus. Narrator: Tommy Wilbanks." Tommy, a preacher's kid from Miss LeFleur's room, slumped in his seat, ears flaming.

"Mary and Joseph: Mary Martha Goode and Skipper Andrews."

Oh, well. I didn't really expect to get Mary.

"The three Wise Men: Andy Cameron, Jeb Mateer, and Duane Hallum."

Jeb shrugged. "What did I tell you?"

"Shepherds: Saranne Russell, Karla Briggs, and Alice Moxley."

Oh, chicken hips! Saranne *and* Karla, the girl who tried to burn Valerie that time in the rest room.

Saranne jumped up, waving her arms. "Miss Gruen, girls can't be shepherds."

"They can this year," Miss Gruen said. "We have more girls than boys. Girls will be shepherds."

Jeb nudged me. "I'll share my beard cotton with you," he offered with a wicked grin.

A beard! No way! Darn old Toad Woman! She could take the fun out of anything, even a Christmas pageant.

"Now, the angel." Miss Gruen paused. The sixth grade leaned forward in their seats. "We selected the person we felt would do the best job."

Debbie looked at her lap, smiling modestly.

"The angel," said Miss Gruen, "will be Valerie Taylor."

Silence. Jeb cracked his knuckles. Then the room exploded.

"Boys and girls, boys and girls." Miss LeFleur clapped her hands, but no one paid attention.

Where *was* Valerie? Alone as usual, two rows behind everyone else. Her face glowed with happiness. And something else, too. Fear?

Andy scowled. "How come Debbie didn't get the angel? I think she sings good."

"Debbie sings very well, indeed," Miss Gruen agreed. "That is why we need her in the chorus."

Debbie burst into baby sobs. "It's not fair. Who ever heard of a nigger angel?"

Saranne leaped up again. "I think we should vote for the angel."

Miss Gruen gave her the toad-eyed stare. "Saranne Russell, this is not a popularity contest. Now, sit."

"No fair," mumbled Saranne, flouncing back in her seat.

I hummed "The First Noel" on the way back to class. For

once, Saranne and the Cheerleaders did not get their way. But they were my friends, weren't they?

I stopped humming, all mixed up again.

December had always been my favorite month. Not this year.

December crawled by, with rehearsal every recess. I hated every minute of it.

Karla pinched me with her pointy fingernails when no one was looking, just for meanness. I pinched her back.

"Was that supposed to hurt, Yankee Girl?" she jeered. My chewed-up nails didn't have the same effect.

"Girls, stop chitchatting and get onstage," ordered Miss LeFleur.

Saranne, Karla, and I slouched onstage to a masking tape X on the floor.

"Where are the sheep?" asked Saranne. "We're shepherds, aren't we?"

"The sheep are imaginary," Miss LeFleur snapped. "Pretend they're in the front row."

"And, lo, the angel of the Lord came upon them, and the glory of the Lord shone round about them: and they were sore afraid," droned Tommy.

"Tommy dear, could you please read with a little more expression?" Miss LeFleur pleaded.

"My daddy says the birth of Jesus don't need no playacting." Tommy shoved his smeary glasses back in place.

"Nobody expects you to be Paul Newman, son," said Miss Gruen from the piano bench. "Just try not to sound like you're calling bus stations."

"Yes, ma'am." Tommy cranked up again, in exactly the same voice. "And the angel said unto them, 'Fear not.'"

Valerie drifted out of the wings.

"Karla dear, could you please look afraid?" sighed Miss LeFleur.

"I am," said Karla. She didn't look afraid; she looked mean. She glared at Valerie, like she might pinch the angel of the Lord.

"Well, try not to look so ferocious." Miss LeFleur got crabbier every day, muttering about how hard the holidays were. Adults were weird. What was so hard about Christmas?

"And the angel said unto them . . ."

"Tommy dear, please don't hold your script in front of your face. We can't hear you," called Miss LeFleur from the back row.

"But I can't read it," Tommy whined. "It's all blurry."

"Why don't you clean your glasses?" sneered Saranne.

Tommy lowered his script an inch. "And the angel said unto them, 'Fear not: for, behold, I bring you good tidings of great joy, which shall be to all people.'"

Miss Gruen's hands hit the opening chord of the angel's solo. Valerie sang in that molasses-and-honey voice:

The first Noel, the angel did say,
Was to certain poor shepherds in fields as they lay . . .

111

The rest of the sixth grade, on risers below the stage, jumped in with the chorus, "Noel, Noel, Noel, Noel, Born is the King of Israel."

Another verse by Valerie, more Tommy. The Wise Men trailed out, late because they'd been arm wrestling backstage. We knelt before the manger, Valerie and the chorus together belted out the last verse, and Leland, the one-boy stage crew, closed the curtains in a cloud of stage dust.

I thought Valerie's solo was the best part of the whole show. I was the only one who did.

"Ain't fair," whined Debbie. "Miss Gruen favored that nigger."

"We oughta do something about it," Saranne chimed in.

"Like what?" said Carrie. "We're just kids."

"What do you think, Yankee Girl?" asked Saranne.

"Well, uh, Debbie does sing good," I stammered. I didn't say that Valerie sang better.

"See? Even Yankee Girl thinks I oughta be the angel," said Debbie. "And I'm *gonna* be the angel."

Debbie said that so often, we all stopped listening. Then one morning, a short woman with a beehive hairdo left our classroom just as we marched in.

"Debbie's mama," said Jeb. "That don't mean anything good."

I found out what it meant at rehearsal that day.

"We have decided to involve more students in the pageant," said Miss Gruen. "So two students will play the angel. Valerie *and* Debbie."

"'Bout time," muttered Andy.

"Valerie will sing from backstage," continued Miss LeFleur. "Debbie will be onstage, mouthing the words. We think this will satisfy everyone."

I didn't know who "everyone" was. Valerie didn't look happy. Neither did Debbie. Only Miss LeFleur looked pleased.

"How come I don't sing?" Debbie pouted. "You said I could be the angel."

"I said you could *be* the angel," said Miss Gruen. "I didn't say you would *sing.*"

Valerie sat stone-faced in the back row, staring straight ahead.

Some kids wore big grins, nudging each other in the side as if to say, "We won!" Mary Martha stared at the floor, embarrassed. Jeb looked disgusted with the whole mess.

"Places, everyone, please." Miss LeFleur clapped her hands.

"Why did Miss Gruen take Valerie's part away from her?" I asked Jeb as we made our way to the stage.

"Andy said that Debbie's mama said if that nigger was the angel, she would 'take care of it.' Debbie's daddy's got buddies in the Klan. Last thing Mr. Thibodeaux and the teachers want is a fuss with the Klan. Anyway, Miss LeFleur thought up the idea of Valerie singing backstage."

If Valerie didn't think it was fair, she never said. Each day she stood offstage and sang the angel's solo, while Debbie mouthed the words.

"Debbie ain't fooling anybody with that sorry act," Karla said.

"It looks tacky," Saranne agreed.

"It's all that nigra's fault." Karla's lip curled.

Wasn't it Debbie's mama's fault? "But—" I began.

"But what?" Saranne and Karla said together.

"Nothing," I muttered, looking away from Karla's fingers.

Who was going to listen to me? I was just the Yankee Girl.

The closer we got to pageant day, the worse things got.

Tommy came down with bronchitis and burst into huge hacking coughs between lines. Miss LeFleur gave him box after box of cough drops. They didn't help Tommy, but at least he shared them.

Karla went right on pinching. I had fingernail cuts all over my hands.

Then there was the day we practiced the curtain call.

"Any questions?" asked Miss LeFleur after we had joined hands and bowed about a million times.

"When does Valerie take her bow?" Mary Martha called out.

Miss LeFleur's face turned Christmas green.

"Oh my," she said in a fake-cheery voice. "We almost forgot Valerie, didn't we? Valerie can stand with the chorus for their bows."

"But, Miss LeFleur—"

Miss LeFleur cut Mary Martha off. "I said Valerie would bow with the chorus. This discussion is over."

Valerie did all the work and Debbie got the curtain call?

The Christmas pageant was turning into one big mess.

Just as big a mess was the class Christmas party.

Miss Gruen stood by her desk, rattling a shoe box.

"Draw your Secret Gift Buddy. Gifts may cost no more than two dollars."

Jeb's hand shot up.

"Miss Gruen, did you separate the boys from the girls? I mean, could a boy get a girl's name?"

"I trust you are mature enough to purchase a gift for a girl if necessary." Miss Gruen fired off her special holiday version of the Look.

"I ain't buying no girl a present," Jeb grumbled.

"And there will be no trading names," added Miss Gruen.

I opened my slip of paper. Carrie. No problem. A Nancy Drew book only cost a dollar ninety-seven, with tax.

I watched the rest of 6B reading their slips. I could tell by their expressions whether they liked their Secret Gift Buddy or not. Saranne looked pleased, Carrie mad, Leland disgusted. Valerie, as usual, stared at the chalkboard, as if there were something more interesting than today's homework assignment written there.

Valerie. Oh no. I knew that whoever got Valerie's name would *not* give her a present. Maybe I could buy two presents and give one to her.

Or maybe the room mothers would bring an extra gift that day. Room mothers made cookies for class parties and chaperoned field trips. They could bring a present for Valerie. But I knew they wouldn't.

I was beginning to see Miss LeFleur's point about Christmas. I wished for the good old days when my biggest problem was which toys to ask for from the Sears Roebuck Christmas catalog. The good old days. Last year.

December glittered with possibilities. Pageants, parties, presents. And at the top of the shining pile, Christmas Day.

Now those same parties, presents, and pageants were booby traps, waiting to explode. I worried all the time. That the pageant would stink. About Karla and her fingernails. That Valerie wouldn't get a present.

What could I do about any of it?

Nothing, that's what. Like Carrie said, we were just kids.

10

NEGROES BOYCOTT DOWNTOWN STORES
Holiday Sales Suffer

★Pageant day, and the whole sixth grade was a nervous wreck. Both classes were penned up in 6B, waiting our turn to go to the auditorium.

The Cheerleaders worked on Debbie's sleep-mashed hairdo with a rat-tail comb and a can of Aqua Net. Tommy paced the edges of the room, mumbling and sucking cough drops. I dodged from corner to corner, avoiding Karla and her iron fingernails.

Only Valerie remained calm, reading at her desk. She was really dressed up, in a red velvet sailor dress with a matching headband. Too bad no one would see her backstage.

Miss Gruen and Miss LeFleur were everywhere at once. Gluing cotton balls to the Wise Men's chins. Tying green crepe-paper bows on the chorus. Making Debbie wipe off her white lipstick. Miss LeFleur looked extra pretty today in a green suit and heels, a cluster of tiny Christmas bells pinned to her shoulder.

Miss Gruen wore her usual brown.

Miss LeFleur fluttered her hands in the air, palms stained green from the crepe paper. "Time to go, boys and girls. Line up, please. Chorus first."

Chattering voices and snatches of Christmas carols from open doors followed us down the hall. The smell of corn-bread dressing wafted from the lunchroom. Lunch.

The scent reminded me that in two hours the Christmas pageant would be over. We'd eat, swap presents, and go home. I tried to remember what life was like before the Christmas pageant.

I couldn't.

We left the chorus at the auditorium door. The rest of us followed Miss LeFleur's clicking heels out the front door, down the sidewalk, and around the corner to the stage door.

Backstage was jammed with first graders in candy-cane costumes and second graders dressed as reindeer. It smelled of stage dust and Pan-Cake makeup.

We were last on the program, which meant standing backstage forever. Tommy paced along the wall, trying not to cough. Mary Martha trailed around in her Mary robes, clutching a Tiny Tears doll wrapped in a blanket that was supposed to be the Baby Jesus. Valerie stood alone, staring into the rafters. Was she nervous? Scared? I was. I could feel sweat circles creeping out from under my arms. I hoped they wouldn't show onstage.

I smelled Miss LeFleur's White Shoulders perfume before I saw her.

"Places, everyone," she stage-whispered over the fifth graders, who were bellowing "God Rest Ye Merry Gentlemen."

Tommy went into a fit of coughs. "It's the dust," he choked. "Anybody got a cough drop?"

"My hair's falling down," whined Debbie.

"You're standing on my robe." Mary Martha shoved Skipper off her hem.

Karla's pinchers closed on the back of my wrist. I scarcely noticed.

Miss LeFleur stepped through the curtains and was almost flattened by the fifth grade stampeding offstage.

"And now," said Miss LeFleur, "the sixth grade presents the Nativity from the Book of Luke."

Feet shuffled on creaking risers as the chorus arranged themselves. Miss Gruen's hands hit the opening chords of "The First Noel." That was Tommy's cue.

He stood in the wings, coughing.

"Go on, man." Jeb shoved him through the curtain.

"And it came to pass in those days . . ." We waited, but Tommy didn't cough.

"Wow," whispered Jeb through his cotton-ball beard. "A Christmas miracle."

The real miracle would be if the sixth grade got through the whole pageant without messing up.

My turn. I clamped my arms over the wet circles and stepped onstage. I peered into the dark, looking for imaginary sheep and Mama. I knew better than to expect Daddy. All I saw were wiggly first-grade candy canes in the front row.

"And they were sore afraid," said Tommy. I gazed up at Debbie the Angel. With her beauty-shop ringlets drooping in her eyes, she looked like a tiny sheepdog.

From the wings, Valerie sang as smooth and sweet as always. If only Debbie had remembered the words she was supposed to mouth. Instead she stared straight at the audience, terrified. She opened and closed her mouth, like a guppy out of water. Then she just stood there, mouth clamped shut. The audience applauded, even if they were left wondering about an angel who sang without opening her mouth.

We shepherds followed Debbie over to the manger. The Wise Men showed up, on time for once. Valerie and the chorus sang the last verse of "The First Noel," Leland yanked the curtain ropes, and it was all over.

I lined up for the curtain call, reaching for Mary Martha's hand. My hand closed on air. No Mary Martha. Where was she? I stepped sideways to take Skipper's hand and close the gap.

"Ready," hollered Leland, and ripped open the curtains.

"Wait," called Mary Martha from backstage.

She ran toward us, towing Valerie. Skipper and I dropped hands to let them in the line. But Mary Martha and Valerie edged past us to the footlights.

"This is Valerie Taylor," Mary Martha said. "She was the voice of the angel."

The applause stopped. There was total, stunned silence.

Then I heard someone clapping. One single person clapping. Then someone else. And someone else.

Not everyone clapped. Debbie's mother slammed her seat shut and left. Some kids booed. Others stomped their feet and whistled. They were probably just happy the program was over.

Valerie's face glowed. I followed her gaze to a Negro man and woman in the front row of the left section, beaming as they applauded. Valerie's parents.

No one else sat in their row.

We returned to 6B after the holiday lunch—stringy turkey and dressing that tasted like mothballs—to find that the room mothers had dropped off the party refreshments. Miss Gruen looked at the plates of cookies and cupcakes, boxes of candy canes, and Hawaiian Punch already poured into Dixie cups.

"Let us commence with the party," said Miss Gruen. She put "Jingle Bell Rock" on the record player. "No dancing," she warned. "This is just party music."

Still, I spied Debbie and Andy doing the twist in a corner of the coatroom. They were the only ones in a party mood.

Kids clumped in corners, mumbling. Over "The Chipmunk Song" I heard snatches of very un-Christmassy conversation.

"Is Mary Martha crazy?"

". . . never thought she was a nigger lover but . . ."

"I'm un-inviting her to my Christmas party . . ."

"Me, too. Mama wouldn't let a nigger lover in the house . . ."

". . . she *touched* a nigra . . ."

Mary Martha stood by the chalkboard, sipping punch. Alone. Her eyes darted around the room. But no one would look at her.

I knew how that felt. Invisible Mary Martha.

"We shall proceed with the gift exchange," Miss Gruen announced.

The green cupcakes and red sugar cookies formed a boulder in my stomach. I hadn't gotten that extra present for Valerie.

Miss Gruen placed a large box covered with brick-printed wallpaper on her desk. I guess it was supposed to be a chimney. Miss Gruen called our names as she pulled packages from the box.

"Alice." My present was small, flat, and light, just the size, shape, and weight of a 45 record. The new Beatles single? Who cared? When would Miss Gruen call Valerie's name?

"Debbie." Debbie ripped open her present as she walked down the aisle, leaving a trail of wrapping paper and ribbon.

"Oooh," she squealed. "Chocolate-covered cherries." Debbie was thrilled. Not only did she know that Andy gave them to her (he told her), but that they had cost three dollars. Andy had left the price tag on the lid.

"Carrie." Carrie hefted the package. "It's a book," she said in a disappointed voice. Oh well. She could always trade.

"Leland." His box contained two handkerchiefs. A good idea, since Leland always wiped his nose on his hand.

"What a lousy present," he said over and over.

Valerie's desk was the only one not covered with Christmas wrap and ribbons. The boulder in my stomach swelled.

"Valerie," Miss Gruen finally called. Relief! She was last, but Valerie had her present. Now I could open my own gift with a clear conscience.

It was a 45 all right. But not the Beatles. "Come See about Me" by the Supremes. I didn't have to look to know that Valerie was watching.

I turned and smiled at her. "Thanks," I said. Everyone was too busy with their own presents to pay us any attention.

She smiled back. "Thought you might want to hear some real music."

"What did you get?" I was happy I could ask the question.

Valerie held up a square ivory-colored paper box, decorated with purple flowers. "Yardley's English Lavender" said the flowing purple script on the sides. Weird. Who would give such an old-lady kind of present?

"Boys and girls, it's time to say thank you," said Miss Gruen. "The giver may identify himself or herself, if they wish."

Up and down the rows, we stood and said "thank you" and "you're welcome." Except for Leland, who said, "Who gave me these stupid hankies?" No one would admit to it.

Valerie stood and softly said, "Thank you for the lavender sachet."

Only she wasn't looking at the class. She was looking at Miss Gruen.

I should've felt happier as we lined up to go home. After all, the pageant had gone okay. Valerie had gotten her curtain call. She even got a present.

But it was Pammie's voice I heard as I watched the class move away from Mary Martha in line.

"Those girls have power." They did.

The Cheerleaders could even make Mary Martha Goode invisible.

11

RESTORED NEGRO CHURCH DEDICATED SUNDAY
Martin Luther King Attends Service

★I lay on my bed New Year's Eve afternoon, reading "Paul and Jane's Fab Christmas" in *16 Magazine*. The Supremes sang "Come See about Me" over and over on the record player.

The phone rang. Probably someone telling us to move back North. Again. Nobody ever called me.

"Alice, phone," Mama yelled.

Me? Who would call me?

"Hey, Alice," rasped a familiar voice. "It's me, Saranne. Watcha doin'?"

Listening to the record Valerie gave me. "Not much." *What do you want?*

"I'm having a spend-the-night party. We're gonna stay up until the New Year. Wanna come?"

"You're having a spend-the-night party," I repeated, just to make sure I wasn't hearing things.

"That's what I said. Can you come?" Saranne sounded like her usual nasty self, but she was inviting me to a party.

"Sure." Mama would say yes. I mean, how many times had I been invited to spend the night this year? Exactly zero, that's how many.

That evening I stood at Saranne's front door, scared and excited at the same time. Saranne could switch from nice to nasty without even breathing hard. But maybe I wouldn't have to worry about that anymore. Because after tonight, I would belong. Really belong.

"C'mon in," Saranne said when she opened the door. "Dump your stuff in the living room."

The other Cheerleaders, minus Mary Martha, sat on the floor around the Russells' aluminum Christmas tree. A twirling light disk at the base clicked and hummed as it changed the silver tree to red, then blue, then green. Pretty. Just not awfully Christmassy.

"Hey, Alice," they called. "Sit on down here. Make yourself to home."

Alice. They called me Alice.

I am inside *the fun, not just watching it. This is the beginning of being friends.*

It was just like spend-the-night parties in Chicago. We popped corn. We polished each other's nails even though we knew our mothers would make us take it off the minute we got home. We listened to the new Beatles record and danced.

Yeah, just like any other spend-the-night. Except that these were the Cheerleaders. And they called me Alice. No one said anything about Yankees.

No one said anything about Mary Martha either until I asked where she was.

"Oh, *her*," sniffed Saranne. "*We* aren't talking to *her*."

"We don't talk to nigger lovers," said Debbie, tossing popcorn in her mouth one piece at a time.

"She *touched* that nigra." Cheryl shuddered. "She *held* her *hand*."

"I hear Mary Martha has a cousin in Ohio. She probably caught some Yankee ideas from her." Carrie made Yankee ideas sound like the measles.

"Oh." What else could I say, without sounding like a Yankee?

Lucky for me, Saranne's mother came in just then to say good night.

"Y'all can stay up until the New Year comes in and that's it," said Mrs. Russell on her way to bed. "I don't want to hear giggling all night."

"We won't, ma'am," we said. We knew we would. That's what spend-the-night parties are for!

"Okay, let's talk," said Saranne as we formed a lopsided circle around her in our sleeping bags. She leaned over and clicked on the radio.

"We've *been* talking," griped Carrie. "I want to listen to the radio. Rebel Radio is counting down the top one hundred songs of the year."

"Not now," said Saranne. "We've got some stuff to figure out." She pitched her voice low under "A Hard Day's Night."

"Like what?" yawned Carrie.

"Like Valerie." Saranne leaned back against the couch, arms folded across her chest.

"Boring," said Debbie. "Let's talk about boys."

"Not now!" said Saranne. "First, we need to get things straight with you, Alice."

Uh-oh. So this was why Saranne invited me. Torture time. How fast can I get dressed and out the door?

"So, Alice." Saranne's voice hurt my ears. "We know you're a Yankee, but are you a nigger lover, too?"

Do I think black people are equal to white people? Of course!
I'd be crazy to say that. Here. Now.

"No," I said, in a voice that sounded very loud to me.

"We don't want any nigger lovers hanging around us." The light wheel changed Saranne's face. Martian green. Spooky blue. Glowing red, like a fun-house monster. "We have to be sure, now that you're one of us."

One of them? That's what she said. One of them. I'll do anything not to be Yankee Girl again.

"Of course I'm not a nigger lover." The word "nigger" felt hard and ugly on my tongue. Like "damn" or "hell" or worse.

It's just a word. I don't mean anything by it.

I couldn't believe I'd said it. But I had.

And that made all the difference.

Everyone chattered at once.

"See, I told you we could trust her . . ."

"Just because her daddy . . ."

"Good thing after that rat fink Mary Martha did what she did . . ."

"See, Alice," Saranne broke in, "we need to all stick together on this Valerie thing. Don't need anybody finking out on us." She helped herself to a handful of popcorn.

"Huh? Finking out about what?" I was lost in this conversation.

"We need to decide what to do about Valerie," said Saranne. "What are we going to do if she goes to junior high with us?"

So what if she does?

But I was one of them now. I kept quiet.

"That would be just terrible," Cheryl mumbled around a mouthful of popcorn.

"Yeah," said Saranne. She crunched her popcorn with her sharp little teeth and swallowed. "What if she brings more of her nigra friends with her? I mean, if she graduates with us, they're gonna think it's okay for them to go to white schools. My daddy says pretty soon the schools will be more nigra than white. If that happens, he's gonna send me to Council School."

"What's Council School?" I said.

"Private school," said Saranne. "The White Citizens' Council started them so we don't have to go to school with nigras."

"Yeah, my daddy says he might send me next year," yawned Debbie. "Big deal. School is school."

"You don't want to go to Council." Saranne poked Debbie

in the arm. "They don't have cheerleaders, because they don't have a football team."

"They *don't*?" Debbie shuddered. "How vomitaceous."

"Get rid of Valerie now, and we won't have to worry about next year." Saranne smacked popcorn salt from her hands.

"How?" said Carrie. "We've tried just about everything and she's still here."

"I don't know," Saranne said. "But we'll think of something."

I felt queasy.

But I'm not doing *anything. I'm just listening.*

Cheryl passed me the popcorn bowl. Debbie rolled my hair on orange-juice cans. And the Beatles sang "She Loves You" as we sat around the Christmas tree and thought of ways to get rid of Valerie Taylor.

In Chicago it was easy to say that Southerners were stupid and wrong. Easy to think that you would do things differently. Not so easy in the Russells' living room. Thinking about what other people should do was one thing. Doing it yourself was another.

We never did come up with a plan for getting rid of Valerie that night. And the first day back from Christmas there was something new to think about.

Seventh grade. Everyone was talking about seventh grade.

Five more months and we would be in junior high. Practically teenagers.

Miss Gruen had seventh grade on the brain, too. "Next year you will change rooms for each class," she said.

I knew that. Pammie said she had five minutes to go to her locker, go to the bathroom, and get to class. It gave me the shivers.

"To accustom you to changing rooms, Miss LeFleur and I will exchange reading groups."

Miss LeFleur at last! Bye-bye, Toad Woman and brown dresses. Hello, Miss LeFleur and pastel sweaters. At least for reading group.

Although the rooms all had the same pale green walls and dirt-colored linoleum, 6A looked cheerier. Potted African violets on the windowsills, a piñata dangling from the ceiling, artwork on the bulletin boards. Miss Gruen tacked perfect spelling and math papers on *her* bulletin boards.

Everyone stampeded for the back seats. Not me. I grabbed the front desk, center row, in front of Miss LeFleur and that big rebel—no—*Confederate* flag.

Today she wore a fluffy mohair sweater that looked like cotton candy. Her charm bracelet jingled as her grading pencil slashed through a pile of tests.

Valerie brushed by my desk on her way up front. She stood before Miss LeFleur, workbook in hand.

Miss LeFleur didn't notice.

Valerie cleared her throat. "Miss LeFleur," she said softly.

The red pencil moved steadily across the page.

"Miss LeFleur," she said in her regular voice.

Miss LeFleur looked up. "Oh! Valerie. I didn't know you were there. Well?" She tapped her pencil on the pile of papers. "What do you want? I'm busy."

Valerie whispered as she pointed to something in the workbook.

"The directions are right there on the page." Miss LeFleur sounded cranky. "I can't be spoon-feeding you. Don't colored schools teach how to read directions?"

"Yes, ma'am." Valerie ducked her head and went back to her desk.

Miss LeFleur opened her bottom desk drawer and got out a spray can of Lysol and a roll of paper towels. Lysol?

Then she stood, stacked the tests on her chair, and sprayed the desk with Lysol, wiping it with a paper towel. When she finished, she sprayed the air around her desk, a magic circle to protect her against . . . Valerie?

"Some folks think nigras have special germs," Jeb explained later. "They don't mean nothing by it."

So why did I have this icky feeling in my stomach? The same feeling I had whenever I looked at Miss LeFleur's Confederate flag.

After lunch that day, Valerie and I were alone in the rest room. All I could think of was Saranne's party.

"You have a good Christmas?" I whacked at my frizzy bangs with a hairbrush, while Valerie washed her hands.

"Hmmm." Valerie smiled at me in the mirror over the sink. "You?"

"Yeah, pretty good." *I went to this party where we figured out ways to get rid of you.* "I've been listening to that record you gave me. I like it."

"The Supremes are great." Valerie dried her hands on a paper towel. "Did you see them on *The Ed Sullivan Show* Sunday night?"

"Yeah," I said. "They did 'Come See about Me.' How come Rebel Radio doesn't play their stuff, if they're that good?"

"I told you if you want *good* music, you listen to WOKJ," Valerie teased.

The bathroom door creaked, and I knew someone was about to come in. I started for the door. Valerie got busy washing her hands. Again.

No one could've told that we had just had a friendly talk, Valerie and I.

Especially not the Cheerleaders.

12

NEGRO LEADERS URGE
STATE COLLEGE INTEGRATION

★Between feeling like a fink and worrying about seventh grade, I didn't notice when Miss Gruen flipped the calendar over to February. Suddenly, Valentine's Day was the number-one topic on the bus.

"We don't have to give valentines to everybody anymore," Saranne rejoiced.

"What do you mean?" I braced as Ralph took a corner on two wheels.

"The other teachers made us give valentines to the whole class." Carrie palmed a peppermint toothpick and passed the bottle to Debbie.

"We're old enough to know who we want to give a valentine to," said Saranne with a pointy-toothed smile.

"Naw, that ain't it." Debbie chewed her toothpick. "I heard

Miss LeFleur say it wasn't fair to make us give a nigra valentines if we didn't want to."

"Who would?" Cheryl hooted.

"Oh, who cares about her," said Debbie. "Andy's going to send me roses." She flipped her wrist so we could all see she was wearing Andy's ID bracelet. It meant they were going steady.

"You lie," snapped Saranne. "He isn't going to do any such thing."

"Is too," said Debbie calmly. "You're just jealous."

I was jealous. A lot of girls wore boys' IDs. Carrie wore Tommy's.

"You don't even like him," Saranne had said when Carrie showed off her new ID bracelet.

"So what?" said Carrie. "It's just until somebody better turns up."

"Like who?" said Saranne in a hateful voice. "Ringo?"

I wasn't sure I even wanted a boyfriend, but if all the Cheerleaders had boyfriends, then I needed one, too. Jeb would do. At least he talked to me. Sometimes.

"No way," said Jeb. We were in the Mateers' den, drawing cloud charts for science. "Why would I give my ID to some old girl?"

"Maybe if you liked somebody . . ." I hinted as I colored cumulonimbus clouds.

"Well, I don't." He rapped out a drum solo on the table edge with colored pencils. "Girls are creepy."

"Gee, thanks." I thumped him on the head with my pencil. I added Valentine's Day to my list of Holidays That Stink.

We stood shivering in the drizzle, waiting for the first bell and the "King Cotton March." It had to be pouring for Mr. Thibodeaux to let us inside before the first bell.

"I've got an idea," Saranne said. "How to get rid of Valerie once and for all." She waited for us to ask her "what."

"What?" asked Cheryl.

"We could send her valentines . . ."

"What!" squawked Debbie.

Saranne gave her a mean look. "I was saying we could send her valentines. But instead of signing our names, we could write stuff like 'Nigger, go home,' 'Niggers stink.' Like that. We can get the whole class to do it."

"The boys won't do it," said Carrie. "Tommy says the boys aren't giving valentines to anybody but their girlfriends."

Saranne waved away the idea like a pesky fly. "The girls will do it."

"Mary Martha won't," Carrie reminded her.

"We aren't talking to her, remember?" said Saranne. "The big nigger lover."

I didn't want to think about valentines at all. When I was in second grade, Daddy got transferred to Chicago the week before Valentine's Day. I sent everyone in the class a card signed, "Your new friend, Alice Moxley." I got one valentine back. From my teacher. Talk about feeling rotten! What if that happened again?

I can't send Valerie a mean card. I'll send a nice one. It'll be our secret.

Saranne didn't waste any time. The drizzle had turned into real rain by recess, so we were stuck inside 6B playing hangman on the chalkboard. While dumb old Leland tried to figure out the word from BIC_CLE, a note flew up and down the aisles. I unfolded the paper triangle and read in Saranne's teeny cursive:

> Do you want Coon Girl and her buddies in OUR junior high? Show her who's boss. Send her a mean valentine. Anybody who doesn't is a niggerlover AND WE KNOW WHO YOU ARE!!!!!!
>
> P.S. No card for Mary Martha Niggerlover either.

I'm sending Valerie a nice card, remember?
AND WE KNOW WHO YOU ARE!!!!!!
In a fog, I moved on to Miss LeFleur's room for reading.

"Alice, would you read next, please?"

"Huh? I mean, ma'am?" I had no idea where we were.

"You need to pay attention, Alice," said Miss LeFleur. She leaned over my shoulder, her charm bracelet jingling as she pointed to my place in the reader. What would Miss LeFleur do if she were me? I'll bet *she* had been popular in the sixth grade. Maybe even a cheerleader.

I stewed about valentines all the way home. I leaped off the bus ahead of Jeb. I didn't want to talk to anybody.

"What's the big hurry?" Jeb fell into step with me. "Whaddya think of that stupid note Saranne sent around about Valerie? Not that I like Valerie or anything," he added quickly. "I wasn't sending valentines nohow."

"What's everybody else going to do?"

Jeb snorted. "Some of the guys are doing it. Some aren't. Leland isn't."

"Really?" I couldn't believe that.

"Yeah. Said he ain't wastin' valentines on no nigger."

That I could believe.

"Hey, there's Andy. See ya." And Jeb took off after his friend.

Wait a minute! Wasn't Jeb the one who told me to just go along? Not to stand up for anybody colored?

I was all mixed up. Again.

Why do you care what Saranne Russell thinks?

Because she can turn me back into Yankee Girl, that's why.

I couldn't send Valerie an ugly valentine. And I couldn't send a nice one. I just wouldn't send one at all.

Okay! All decided!

Then why did I wake up every hour all night long? Midnight, said my clock radio. One o'clock, two. I flipped my pillow looking for a cool spot. Three o'clock, four. The clock radio popped on at six-thirty. The Beatles sang "I Feel Fine."

I sure didn't.

Friday, the day of the party, the Cheerleaders bounced in their bus seats, full of the Plan.

Saranne shook her grocery sack of valentines. "I can't wait to see you-know-who's face."

I could wait.

There was an empty spot on the backseat.

"Where's Carrie?" I asked.

Saranne rolled her eyes and frowned. "Sitting down front. She's in mourning."

"Mourning? Gee, who died?"

"Nobody. Ringo got married yesterday." Debbie smacked her lime Fruit Stripe and rolled her eyes.

Carrie got off the bus with the rest of us, head down, feet dragging. Everyone else was all keyed up. The girls giggled and pretended to ignore the boys.

The boys didn't have to pretend; they *were* ignoring the girls. Most of them were empty-handed, except Andy, who lugged a Kennington's shopping bag.

"That's a lot of valentines," Debbie hinted, trying to peek in the bag.

"No fair looking." Andy hefted the bag out of Debbie's reach.

"Where are your valentines?" I asked Jeb as we marched in.

"Told you I wasn't giving any," he said. He wasn't kidding.

Chicken hips!

Miss Gruen made us put our cards in our cubbies. "I don't want y'all fiddling with those cards all morning," she said.

Lined up on the wide windowsill were our valentine mailboxes—foil-covered shoe boxes. My head hurt just looking at them. I wished the day was over.

I wish I were in Cuba. I'll bet they don't even have Valentine's Day.

Recess, reading, lunch.

I didn't do anything wrong.

Social studies, spelling, English.

I should've stopped them.

The room mothers arrived with the refreshments: pink heart-shaped cookies and cans of Hawaiian Punch. Party time. I was not in a party mood.

I got the sack of cards from my cubby and stuffed them into the mailboxes. I couldn't wait for this party to be over.

Saranne winked as she passed me on my way back to my desk. I looked away.

"Class, you may get your boxes," announced Miss Gruen.

I stared at my box, afraid to touch it. Maybe it was empty.

Serve you right. You should've tried to stop them.

I peeked under the lid. Not empty. About ten cards, including a big one.

Good old Jeb! Who else could have sent a card this big? That old faker had fibbed to me!

Andy marched down the aisle with his Kennington's bag, thrust it at Debbie, and took off back to his seat. Debbie pulled out a heart-shaped box of chocolate-covered cherries and three slightly droopy roses in green florist paper.

"My first roses," she sighed.

"Huh," said Saranne. "Those old roses are practically dead."

"Are not." Debbie made a big deal of sniffing the flowers. "They still smell."

Valerie sat, hands folded, box unopened on her desk. I was afraid to watch her.

I turned back to my valentines. I picked up the big one, then decided to save it till last. I opened a card from Mary Martha. She'd probably sent one to everyone. I remembered that I hadn't sent *her* one.

"Valerie's opening her box," Carrie whispered. "Pass it on."

I didn't have to. All eyes watched Valerie.

I didn't want to look. But I had to.

Valerie picked up the first envelope. We all held our breath. She pulled out a medium-sized card, read the message, then turned it over. Valerie caught Mary Martha's eye and smiled. Mary Martha smiled back.

"Nigger lover," muttered Debbie.

Valerie pulled out another card and . . . nothing happened. She didn't smile, didn't frown, didn't blink. Didn't cry. Another card. Same thing.

"What's with that girl?" said Carrie under her breath. "Why isn't she boohooing?"

Valerie opened fifteen more envelopes. Then she scooped them back into the box, closed the lid, and sipped her Hawaiian Punch.

Everyone in 6B sat stunned for a moment. Then, slowly, the room came back to life. A low buzzing of voices and sideways looks at Valerie. Kids wandered up and down the aisles, comparing cards. Saranne strolled by my desk.

"Well, that was a great big nothing," she said, lip curled. "We'll have to think of something else." She pointed to the big envelope. "You going to open that?"

"Later." I made sure snoopy old Saranne was talking to

Cheryl before I did. I held it in both hands, almost afraid to open it. Suddenly, I wasn't sure I wanted Jeb as a boyfriend. Could you trade stamps with a boyfriend?

I took a deep breath.

Here goes nothing.

A big gold card, decorated with fake red velvet to look like the ace of hearts. "You're Aces with me, Valentine," in glittery script. On the back, in perfect Palmer penmanship, "Valerie."

At least I didn't send her a mean card.

I glanced over at Valerie, to smile my thanks.

Valerie stared at her lap, biting her lower lip. And I knew. Knew it hadn't been enough to not follow the crowd. I should've done the Right Thing. I should've sent her that card.

I counted up the people I'd fooled into thinking I was a nice person. My parents, Jeb, Valerie. I fooled everyone.

Everyone but me. And right this minute, I hated me.

13

FEDERAL GOVERNMENT SUES TO
INTEGRATE EATING PLACES

★Valerie was absent the next Monday.

"We did it." Saranne flashed her pointy-toothed grin. "She's gone back to wherever she came from."

"She might just be absent," Carrie pointed out.

"She's *never* absent," Saranne said in her bossiest voice.

There were worse things than being Invisible Alice or Yankee Girl. Like being a fink. A no-good fink, who didn't have any guts.

After supper that night, I sat at the breakfast bar, staring at my math homework but thinking about Valerie.

The phone rang.

"It's for you." Mama handed me the receiver and tactfully left the room.

"Hey, Alice. It's Valerie."

"Hey. We missed you at school today." Which was a big, fat lie, but that's what you were supposed to say. It was manners.

"Thanks." Valerie knew about manners, too. "I had the stomach bug."

"Oh." Relief! So she hadn't gone back to her old school. "You feeling better?"

"Yeah. I'll be back tomorrow. That's why I'm calling. To see if we have any math homework."

"Yeah. I've got it right here." I told her the page number and which problems we were supposed to work.

"Thanks," said Valerie.

"You're welcome." Silence hummed across the phone line. Valerie was the one who called, so she was the one who was supposed to say goodbye. It was manners.

"I didn't really have the stomach bug," Valerie said.

"You didn't?"

"Oh, I threw up all right, but it wasn't any old bug. It's 'cause I was scared."

"What're you scared of?" I could think of about a hundred things Valerie had to be scared of.

"My daddy's going over to Alabama with Dr. King. Help signing folks up to vote. Someplace called Selma, in a couple weeks. White people over there are crazy. All the time beating and shooting folks. I don't want Daddy to go." Valerie's voice grew smaller and smaller until she was whispering. I sounded the same way when I was trying not to cry.

146

"Why don't you ask him not to go?" I said. "It's not like it's his paying job. Working for Dr. King, I mean."

"I know." Valerie sighed. "But Daddy says that we'll be paid a thousand times over when we get our equal rights."

"What's he mean by that?"

"I reckon he means that we won't have to think all the time whether we can go here or there or do this or that. White people don't think about whether or not they're allowed in some place, do they?"

"No." It never crossed my mind that I might be in the wrong place because of my color. Well, except for that day at the football game. "Do you think about it a lot?"

"Yeah. But sometimes I just forget. Like last summer. Our family drove all the way to New York City to visit kin. Every time we needed to go to the bathroom, we had to stop the car and go in an empty Crisco can in the backseat."

"Why didn't you just go to a filling station? They aren't the cleanest bathrooms in the world, but it's better than a Crisco can."

"'Cause white filling stations in the South won't let Negroes use their bathrooms, that's how come. There's never a colored station around when you need one."

"Oh." I never thought about that.

"It was all on account of the pie."

"Pie?" That didn't make any sense. Maybe Valerie was sick after all.

"We were someplace in Kentucky, and we saw this sign in a

window of a bus-station lunch counter. It said FRESH HOME-
MADE PIES. We'd been eating Vienna sausages out of the can
and crackers, 'cause that stuff don't spoil in the car. Suddenly,
all we could think about was those pies.

"Daddy said, 'Lots of Negroes come through here on the
bus. I'll bet they'll serve us.'"

"Did they?"

"I'm telling a story here," said Valerie, so I knew that I wasn't
supposed to interrupt. "First, we looked for a WHITES ONLY
sign. We didn't see one, so we walked in. The place was empty,
except for a gray-haired white lady behind the counter. Daddy
asked if they served Negroes.

"'Why, sure,' said the white lady. 'What y'all going to have?'

"I felt so special. I'd never eaten at a lunch counter with
twirly stools before. I didn't notice that the window screens
were busted and there were flies all over. I didn't see that the
dishes were cracked and nasty brown, like somebody been using them for ashtrays. I didn't see all that until later.

"All I saw was that glass pie case on the counter. It was lit up
like a jewelry-store window, with pies on shelves turning slow
under the lights. Each one looked like the best kind of pie in
the world. I picked coconut. Lucy wanted chocolate.

"The lady took our pie slices behind the counter. She had
her back to us, so I couldn't see what she was doing. But when
she brought our pies to us, I could see she had put whipped
cream on them.

"'We didn't ask for whipped cream,' Daddy said. 'How

much extra does that cost?' I knew we didn't have any extra money.

"'Nothing a'tall,' said the lady. 'My treat. Now, them pies cost one dollar.' Daddy paid her and she brought us our forks.

"I looked at my coconut pie, all golden and crispy under that fluffy cream, and decided to take little bitty bites, to make it last longer.

"Good thing, 'cause when I put that pie in my mouth, something happened. I tasted sweet cream, and crunchy coconut, and then the worst taste I'd ever tasted. Mama and Daddy had funny looks on their faces. They put down their forks. Mama pinched Lucy's leg under the counter, so's she wouldn't spit out her pie.

"'Just swallow it,' Daddy said in my ear. 'Don't give that lady satisfaction.'

"I swallowed. 'What is it?' I whispered. I wanted water bad, but the lady hadn't given us any.

"'Salt,' Daddy whispered back. 'She put salt over the tops of these pies and covered it up with the whipped cream. Let's just go.' We stood up.

"'What's the matter? Didn't you like my pies?' the lady said. 'It's my special recipe for niggers.' She smiled. I didn't know a smile could be ugly.

"I wanted to smash my pie in her face. But Daddy said, 'Keep walking. Don't look back.'

"The lady called after us, 'You be sure and tell all your friends how we treat niggers here.'"

Another humming silence. Through the receiver I heard a woman call, "Valerie! You hang up that phone right now and get to your homework."

"In a minute, Mama," Valerie yelled back. Then not yelling, "I gotta go now, Alice. Thanks for telling me about the math. See you tomorrow."

Click. The dial tone buzzed in my ear.

It was going to take more than Saranne Russell and the Cheerleaders to get rid of Valerie Taylor.

A lot more.

That night, I dreamed about Emmett Till again.

"What are you doing here?" I asked. But he acted like he didn't hear. He had something to say.

"What do you think would've happened if just one white person had stood up for me?"

"You'd still be alive," I said.

"Maybe," he said, his eyes round and sad. "Or maybe that white person be dead, too."

14

JACKSON DAILY JOURNAL, Saturday, March 6, 1965

CIVIL RIGHTS LEADERS PLAN MARCH
TO ALABAMA CAPITOL

★Spring came early in the South. Chicago in March was snow pants, snow boots, and piles of dirty snow. Mississippi in March was shorts and azaleas and biking to the Tote-Sum for ICEEs.

I sat cross-legged on the den floor, warm breezes from the screen door tickling my neck as I traced a map of Mexico for social studies. Mrs. Mateer perched on the couch, visiting while Mama ironed.

"Y'all aren't moving, are you?" Mrs. Mateer dug her cigarettes and lighter out of her shorts pocket. "Y'all just got here."

"Lord, no." Mama dampened Daddy's shirt with the sprinkler bottle. "What makes you ask?" A puff of steam rose where the hot iron touched the wet shirt.

Mrs. Mateer tapped a cigarette out of her pack. "Coupla fellas in a pink Cadillac took pictures of your house while y'all were out the other day." She flicked the lighter. "Real estate folks have big cars." She blew a smoke ring, putting a period on her sentence.

"Those weren't Realtors," Daddy said at supper. "They were Klan. I saw the car when I came in tonight."

"What? Why?" I said. The Klan! Right in front of our house, again!

"They're keeping track of us," Daddy chuckled.

"What's so funny?" I said. I didn't think the Klan was a bit funny.

"A pink Cadillac." Daddy laughed. "The whole point of a stakeout is *not* being seen. You don't sit in a pink Cadillac in broad daylight!" He shook his head. "Oh well, as long as those old boys are just shooting cameras, we're okay. I hope they get some good snaps of me taking out the garbage."

"Why don't we call the police?" I asked.

"Well, Pookie, those fellas aren't breaking any laws, just taking pictures. They'll go away eventually. They won't hurt us. I promise."

But they didn't go away. When I came home a few days later, the Cadillac was there, but Mama wasn't. The empty carport meant Mama was running errands. I got the house key from under the doormat and let myself in.

Every sound seemed a thousand times louder in the empty house. I clicked on the kitchen radio and tuned it to WOKJ. The Supremes sang "Stop! In the Name of Love," drowning out the noises. I danced through the living room to my room, closing the curtains so I wouldn't see the Cadillac.

Dead air followed the Supremes. Maybe the deejay went to the bathroom. The windows rattled in the warm March wind. The house creaked. The refrigerator hummed loudly. I had my hand on the radio dial to change to Rebel Radio when . . .

Thunk! Something hit the living room window.

A bomb?

I had to escape!

But where? I knew the Mateers had gone shopping.

I peeked out my bedroom window. The men in the Cadillac looked asleep, but they didn't fool me. They had probably thrown a Molotov cocktail, a bomb made with gasoline and a pop bottle. It just hadn't gone off. Yet.

Maybe Jeb was home now. With a shaking finger, I dialed his number.

I always let the phone ring ten times because maybe the person was in the bathroom. I counted thirty-six rings. The Mateers weren't home.

Trapped. Windows in every room. Was there no safe place in the house?

The closet. My bedroom closet.

I checked out front. One of the Cadillac men leaned against the hood, smoking a cigarette. What would he do next?

I slid open the closet door and dived in, pushing away a pile of shoes. I shoved at the skirts dangling in my face. The closet smelled like sweaty sneakers and mothballs. At least the Klan couldn't get me. Could they?

The house settle-creaked in the wind. Or was someone trying to get in the house? I couldn't tell, because right then WOKJ came back on the air.

Over the distant mumble of the radio, I could hear the door from the kitchen into the carport opening. I hadn't locked it behind me. How stupid could I be? Was it the guy with the cigarette?

Whonk! Something heavy landed on the kitchen counter. A gun? Would Mama find my bullet-riddled body spilling from the closet?

"Alice Ann Moxley," a voice bellowed from the kitchen. "You march yourself out here right this minute."

Mama! The something heavy was her wooden purse hitting the counter. I pushed open the closet door and gulped fresh air.

Mama started right in. "You know better than to leave doors unlocked."

I started babbling about noises and pink-Cadillac men.

"Calm down," said Mama. "Something hit the living room window? Well, let's go see what it is."

"I'm not going out there." Not as long as the Cadillac was parked in front.

"It was a robin," Mama said when she came back. "The poor thing flew into the window. I found him dead in the gardenia bushes. You were scared of a dead bird."

Well, it *could* have been a bomb. I was never staying in the house alone again.

A couple of nights later, Daddy came home only long enough to eat.

"I have to go back to work." He shoveled creamed corn onto his plate.

"Nice of you to drop in." Mama's lips flattened as she speared a ham slice with a serving fork.

Oh, chicken hips. Mama and Daddy were going to fight. Time to change the subject.

"Valerie's daddy is in Alabama with Martin Luther King. Someplace called Selma." Valerie always got Daddy's attention. This time it backfired.

"You want to know why I work seven days a week, twelve hours a day?" Daddy sliced his ham into precise squares. "People like Dr. King and Reverend Taylor. To protect their rights."

"Why can't you protect their rights from nine to five?" Mama spooned corn on her plate with an angry splat. "Why do you have to go in tonight?"

"Inspector Ryan is here from headquarters." Daddy checked his watch, then pushed back his chair from the table. Mama scowled as she followed him out to the car.

I cleared the table, clashing silverware and plates as I stacked them on the drain board. I didn't want to hear what was going on outside. Not that they would have a big fight in the driveway, where the neighbors could see them.

No, they would be superpolite to each other the way that people are when they *actually* hate each other's guts. Mama thought yelling was "unpleasant."

I wondered if Daddy really was meeting with the inspector,

or if he was doing something more dangerous. The bad thing about an FBI agent father was that you never knew where he was or what he was doing. He wasn't supposed to talk about work, so I knew better than to ask him. He might be sitting in his office writing reports. Or he might be out in the country somewhere tracking down KKKers. You just didn't know.

For the millionth time, I wished that Daddy sold shoes or drove a milk truck. A job where you couldn't get killed by the Klan.

Mama was still grouchy from the fight when she drove me to Dr. Warren's after school the next day.

"Working sixty, seventy hours a week," she grumbled. "Even Martin Luther King takes a day off now and then." She griped all the way to the doctor's office and all the way home.

We could hear our phone ringing when we pulled into the carport. Mama ran in to answer it.

Jeb was in his driveway shooting baskets. "Wanna play horse?" he called.

"Sure. Let me put my books in the house."

Mama hung up the phone as I came in. "I'm going to pick up Daddy. Do you want to come with me?"

And listen to her gripe some more? I shook my head. "I'm going over to Jeb's."

"All right. We'll be back in half an hour." I was out the kitchen door before she finished her sentence. Mama fired up the Chrysler and drove away as Jeb tossed me the basketball.

I lost two games in a row.

"Play again?" Jeb spun the ball in his hands.

"Kind of dark, isn't it?" I squinted at my Timex. Six-fifteen? That couldn't be right! "Mama should be home by now." I tried not to sound scared.

Mrs. Mateer stuck her head out the kitchen door. "Supper, son."

"Alice's mama's gone to fetch her daddy and they ain't home yet," Jeb said. "She's kinda worried."

Mrs. Mateer could tell I didn't want to be alone because she said I could stay with them until Mama and Daddy got home.

"Why don't you call the office, hon?" she said. "Your daddy might be detained at work."

"Federal Bureau of Investigation, how may I help you?" It was Grady, one of the clerks. For some reason, the FBI clerks were always called by their first names, instead of "mister."

"Grady, this is Alice Moxley." It felt good to hear a familiar voice. "Has my father left yet?"

"Let me check." I heard the phone receiver clunk on the desk and Grady walking away. Then footsteps coming back.

"Alice, you still there? He clocked out at 5:20. He isn't home yet?"

Almost an hour ago! My stomach turned to ice.

"I haven't looked in a while," I said. "I'm over at the neighbors'."

"I see." A long humming silence. "Well, they might be home now and wondering where *you* are," Grady said in a fake cheerful voice. "But, Alice . . ."

"Yeah, Grady?"

"If they don't turn up soon, give me a call, okay? I don't want you to be there alone."

I hung up.

"He left already." I tried not to cry in front of the Mateers, eating their supper at the breakfast bar. "Maybe they're home by now. I'll go look."

They weren't.

"I'll make a few phone calls," said Mrs. Mateer in a take-charge voice. "Jeb, Pammie, take Alice home and stay with her."

"I can't. I'm baby-sitting, remember?" A car honked in the driveway as Pammie gathered up her schoolbooks. "Don't worry, Alice. Your parents are fine." She gave my arm a squeeze on her way out.

Jeb and I stepped out into the warm, windy night. The air smelled like damp earth and azaleas. A full moon glowed in a star-flecked sky. Such a soft spring night. For a minute, I felt happy.

Then I looked across the street. The pink Cadillac was gone. Of course it was gone. Those guys were off kidnapping my parents.

My stomach hurt.

I unlocked the back door and fumbled for the light switch. Even with the lights on, the rooms had a spooky, empty feeling. Jeb flopped on the den couch, air whooshing out of the vinyl cushions.

"*The Beverly Hillbillies* is on," he said. "Wanna watch?"

"I don't care." I turned on the TV, and canned laughter filled the room. "Jeb, what'll I do if they're dead?"

He leaned back and stared at the ceiling. "Skipper's mama died last year. Our class took up money for funeral flowers. Everyone was extra nice to him. For about a week."

Life without Mama and Daddy? I couldn't imagine it. I didn't *want* to imagine it.

"This is a dumb show," griped Jeb. He twisted the TV dial to the other channel. "Nothing on." He wandered into the living room.

I joined him there and pressed my forehead against the cool window glass. Who would tell me my parents were dead. Grady? The police? Mrs. Mateer?

"Hey, Alice," Jeb said softly. "Don't worry. They'll be okay. You'll see." He sounded so gentle and un-Jeb-like that it scared me.

He thinks they're dead, too.

Far down the street, the bobbing headlights of a car came toward us, passing under a streetlight. The Chrysler. My parents were home.

"See? I told you they'd be okay." Jeb sounded like Jeb again. He let himself out as the Chrysler bumped into the driveway.

I yanked open the driver's door before Daddy turned the motor off.

"Where have you been?" I burst into tears. "I thought you were dead!"

"Where have *you* been, young lady?" said Mama. "We called and called."

"I was at the Mateers'," I blubbered. "Why didn't you call there?"

"We did," said Daddy. "The line was busy. Then when we got through, there was no one home to answer the phone."

"Why didn't you call somebody else?" I hollered.

"Who?" demanded Mama. "Just who else could we have called?"

She had a point. "You're four hours late!" I yelled, to change the subject.

"We had a little emergency," said Daddy. "Inspector Ryan's ulcer kicked up so we took him to the hospital. We didn't think it would take so long for a doctor to see him. I'm sorry." Daddy hugged me close. "I promise you, nothing will happen to us."

You can't promise that. You don't know what's going to happen. Nobody knows what's going to happen.

It was weird knowing Daddy had made a promise he couldn't keep. Like I'd grown up all in a minute. I didn't want to be a grownup. Not yet.

The following Monday, Valerie and Lucy arrived at school in a strange car driven by a strange woman. As she passed me on the playground, I could see that Valerie's eyes were wet and red. Something terrible must have happened. Valerie never cried.

I looked around. The Cheerleaders had their heads buried

in *Song Hits,* memorizing the Beatles' newest, "Eight Days a Week." The coast was clear.

"Hey, Valerie." I touched her elbow. "Anything wrong?"

"Daddy's been arrested." She looked down at the asphalt. "There was a march yesterday and they arrested everybody. He's in jail."

Arrested! What did you say to someone whose daddy was in jail? I decided on "Gee, that's too bad."

Valerie whirled to face me, chin up, eyes flashing.

"No, it's not," she said. "It's an honor."

"What did he do?" I'd never heard of a minister getting arrested.

Valerie's eyes lost their flash and just looked sad. "He got arrested at the march in Alabama yesterday. He promised nothing would happen to him." Her lip quivered.

"I'm sorry," I said, but Valerie wasn't listening. She stared at Miss LeFleur on the steps, taking the "King Cotton March" out of the record jacket.

"Daddy came home Friday, just for the day. You know what we did Friday night?" Valerie's voice sounded far away. "Daddy and me? We watched *The Addams Family* on TV. That's our favorite show. We hardly ever get to watch it together 'cause Daddy's hardly ever home. But he was home Friday night. We made popcorn and watched *The Addams Family.* Lucy was asleep and Mama was at a meeting, so it was just him and me. He sure likes that show. His favorite character is Cousin Itt. We laughed our heads off."

It was hard to imagine the Reverend Taylor laughing his head off. I always pictured him like he was on the news, solemn-faced in a suit and tie. Did he wear sport shirts at home and walk around in his socks, the way my daddy did?

I stared at the back of Valerie's neck as we marched into school.

I realize now we have something else in common, Valerie. We're scared for our daddies.

Because eleven-year-old girls have no say in what happens to their daddies. No matter what kind of promises those daddies make.

15

STATE OFFICIALS SAY VOTER RIGHTS BILL WORK OF NEGRO TROUBLEMAKERS

★The pink Cadillac moved on.

"I told you we were too boring for the Klan," said Daddy. "They won't be back."

Still, I checked the street every night before I went to sleep.

After all, there are things that daddies couldn't promise.

I watched Valerie. She didn't look like somebody whose daddy was in jail. She stood for the Pledge, sat for the Lord's Prayer, and answered Miss Gruen when she was called on. Same as always. Only her bit-up fingernails gave her away. Valerie Taylor was one cool customer.

I wished I could tell her that.

"I can't wait for Class Day," said Cheryl.

"What's Class Day?" I asked. "Is that like graduation?"

"Sort of," said Carrie. "Except that it's before the end of the year, and we don't get diplomas. It's a program to show our parents what we've learned. And they hand out some awards. It's a very big deal."

"I can't wait for the Class Day *party*," said Debbie. "Even if Mary Martha *is* giving it."

"Not that we *like* that nigger lover," explained Saranne. "But I want to go to her party."

As soon as Mary Martha and Skipper announced they were throwing a graduation party, the Cheerleaders made up to Mary Martha. If it had been me, I would have been so happy that they were talking to me again, I'd have tap-danced on the ceiling. Not Mary Martha. She was her usual calm, polite self.

"My cousin's band, the Walloos, is going to play," she told us. "They know all the Beatles songs." She showed us an invitation.

Mary Martha Goode and Skipper Andrews invite you
to a party in honor
of the Parnell School Class of 1965
Friday, May 7, 1965
6:00 until 10:30 p.m.
Eastlake Country Club
Dress: Semiformal
R.S.V.P.

"What does semiformal mean?" asked Debbie.

"It means what you wear to Class Day," said Mary Martha.

Miss Gruen had already spelled out what to wear Class Day.

"Sunday-school clothes. Boys: jackets and ties, dress shoes. Girls: pastel dresses, white shoes." She gave us the Look, daring us to show up in shorts and sneakers.

We compared Class Day dresses at recess.

"Mine came from Memphis and, boy, was it expensive," bragged Saranne. "It's yellow and has ribbon stripes up the front."

"Mama bought mine at Kennington's," said Mary Martha. "It's pink."

"Hope somebody tells ol' Valerie what pastel means," said Saranne. "Be just like a nigra to show up in a red dress. They do like bright colors."

That's not so. Valerie wears pastel dresses all the time.

I opened my mouth, then closed it.

I worried that Mama would sew my Class Day dress. I didn't want to go through *that* again.

Instead, we went to La Petite, a fancy girls' store next to Dr. Warren's. Mama gasped at the price tags, but said, "The sky's the limit. You only graduate from sixth grade once." She smiled and added, "I hope!"

I pulled out every size-eleven pastel dress on the rack, while Mama watched from a gilt-and-brocade armchair. A saleslady with silver hair in a French knot hovered over us. She hinted that powder blue was my color, and that perhaps yellow was not. Such a nice lady, in her tailored navy dress and high heels and expensive-smelling perfume.

Especially since Mama and I weren't dressed for shopping in such a fancy place. My plaid skirt was safety-pinned at the waist where I'd popped a button. Mama wore a denim skirt, a bandanna-print blouse, and red Keds. And bobby socks! *Nobody* wore bobby socks!

The doorbell pinged softly. A dressed-up Negro woman and a girl my age entered the store.

I didn't pay them much attention as I twirled before the three-way mirror. I had found the perfect dress, powder blue with an Empire waist and forget-me-nots embroidered on the bodice. I was sure Jane Asher had one just like it.

As I admired myself, the Negro girl clicked hangers back and forth on the rack. Maybe she was looking for a Class Day dress, too.

"Oh Mama, I love this one." She pulled out a hanger with a pink lace shift.

The saleslady was at the girl's side in a flash. I didn't know you could move that fast in three-inch heels.

"Shall I ring it up for you?" she said. It wasn't what she said, but how she said it. Polite but cold. Real cold.

The Negro woman shook her head. "She'll try it on first. Where are your dressing rooms?"

The saleslady's smile froze. "We have no dressing rooms."

I thought she was joking. After all, there I stood in a dress with a big price tag dangling from the sleeve.

"That girl is trying on a dress," said the Negro girl, looking at me.

"I said, we do not have dressing rooms," repeated the saleslady, no longer smiling. "Now, do you want the dress or not?"

"Put the dress back, Demetria," said the girl's mother.

"No need." The saleslady swept the dress from the girl's hands, returning it to the rack with a sharp click of the hanger. "Good afternoon," she said in a frosty voice, ushering the mother and daughter out the door.

The saleslady turned toward us, smile back in place.

"I'm so sorry," she fluttered. "Honestly, nigras think they can shop anywhere."

"Can't they?" Mama's eyebrows met in a single line.

"I suppose," said the saleslady. "But now they think they can try on clothes in the store."

"What's wrong with that?" Mama said.

The saleslady gave Mama a long look. "I can tell y'all aren't from around here. I suppose up North nigras do as they please, but not here. Would you buy a dress a nigra tried on?"

Mama got to her feet. "Alice, take the dress off. We're leaving."

"But Mama . . ."

"We're going to a store where everyone is treated the same," said Mama.

The saleslady smiled unpleasantly. "Then you'll have to travel a ways. There's not a white store in the state of Mississippi that lets colored try on clothes. If they want to try on clothes, they can go down to Farish Street, to the nigra stores."

"And I don't suppose they're allowed to return clothes, are they?"

"Of course not. Who would . . ."

"Yes, I know. Who would buy something worn by a Negro." Mama looked at me. "Alice?"

I was supposed to say I didn't want the dress. But I did. It was the most perfect dress in the world and I wanted it.

Bye-bye, perfect Jane Asher dress.

"I can wear my Easter dress," I sighed as I trudged back to the dressing room.

Mama waited until we pulled out of the store parking lot before she said, "I'm really proud of you, Alice."

I knew I had done the Right Thing, but it didn't make me feel one bit better. I didn't want to be the only girl without a new dress for Class Day. My Easter dress was a hand-me-down from one of my cousins. A hand-me-down didn't make me feel like Jane Asher.

If a secondhand dress wasn't enough to worry about, the Cheerleaders had dates for the party.

"Our first girl-boy party," Debbie said. "Andy is taking me. Our first date," she sighed with a sappy look on her face.

Date? Sixth graders with *dates*?

It looked that way. Carrie and Tommy. Mary Martha and Skipper. Every day someone else announced they had a date for the party. Even Saranne said she was going with Duane. She was welcome to the old nose-picker!

"She probably asked him herself," said Carrie as Saranne moved off to brag to another group.

A girl ask a *boy*? Great idea!

Later that afternoon, as Jeb and I rode our bikes to the Tote-Sum, I asked him, "You taking anybody to the Class Day party?"

"Are you nuts? I'm not even going to that sorry old party."

"How come? Skipper and Andy and Tommy and even old Duane are going. With girls."

"Who wants to dance with *girls*?"

"You don't have to dance. We could go together. Goof around, do stuff." I acted like we'd just be buddies, going to a dumb old party.

"No way!"

Drastic measures were needed. I needed a Plan.

The next afternoon, I knocked on the Mateers' back door, then let myself in, like always.

I walked into the middle of World War Three.

"I ain't going, and you can't make me," said Jeb. He slouched on the den couch, Mrs. Mateer and Pammie looming over him.

"Hey, Alice," said Pammie. "You're just in time to talk some sense into my dumb brother. He says he's not going to the Class Day party."

"Well, I ain't!" Jeb folded his arms and glared at all three of us. "I'll have to wear a jacket and tie and dance and I ain't going," he said in one big breath.

"You want to ride over with me?" I said, as if I had just thought of it.

"Uh-uh. No way."

"You are such a social reject," said Pammie, rolling her eyes.

Mrs. Mateer nudged Pammie. "Let Alice and Jeb talk in private." Jeb's mother winked at me on her way out.

Jeb gave me the fisheye. "Ain't going."

"Everybody else is. Andy's going. Skipper's giving it. With Mary Martha, I mean."

"Yeah, and they're bringing *girls*."

Time for the Plan.

"Remember back last fall when you said you owed me one? Well, this is the one you owe me. You take me to the party."

Jeb turned white under his tan. "No way. I mean, really, no way!"

"All right for you, Jeb Stuart Mateer," I said in a huff. "I'll tell everybody you're a big, fat promise breaker."

Jeb thought for a minute. "How 'bout a contest? You win, I'll take you. I win, I don't."

I swallowed my grin. Things were going according to the Plan.

"Okay," I said. "But I get to pick the contest."

Jeb looked suspicious. "Like what?"

"Wrestle you for it."

Jeb grinned. "Sure. When do you want to do it?"

"Right now." Before Jeb could move, I judo-flipped him to the floor and sat on his chest. "I win!" An FBI agent father sometimes came in handy. Especially one who taught you judo.

"No fair!" Jeb hollered loud enough for Pammie and Mrs. Mateer to come running.

"What's wrong, son?" said Mrs. Mateer as I got off Jeb's chest.

Jeb and I told her, stepping on each other's words. Somehow, she got the picture.

"Did you really promise to take Alice if she won?"

Jeb fiddled with a loose shirt button.

"Did you? Jeb Stuart Mateer, you look at me when I speak to you." Mrs. Mateer grabbed his chin, forcing him to look at her.

"Yes, ma'am, but . . ."

"Either you did or you didn't. Did you?" Mrs. Mateer let go of Jeb and reached for her cigarettes.

"Yes, ma'am." Jeb studied the toes of his loafers.

"Then you're taking her." Mrs. Mateer lit a cigarette, blew a smoke ring, and that was that.

I had a date! Everything was terrific.

For about two hours.

Daddy studied the invitation over supper. "Is your whole class invited to this party?"

"I guess so." Who cared? *I* was invited!

"Even Valerie Taylor?"

"I don't know. Why?"

"Negroes aren't allowed in country clubs."

"Then I guess she wasn't invited."

171

So what else is new?

"Do you think it's right that these kids invited everyone except Valerie?" Daddy looked me in the eye. I looked away.

"Gee, Daddy, it's their party. They can invite who they want."

"You ask if Valerie is invited," said Daddy. "Then I want you to think seriously about this."

I snagged Mary Martha on the playground before school.

"No," she said, her eyes troubled. "Negroes aren't allowed in the country club. Valerie would feel out of place. There won't be anyone for her to dance with."

Of course! In a way, Mary Martha was doing Valerie a favor. Valerie wouldn't have a good time.

Daddy didn't see it that way at all.

"I could tell you that you can't go," he said in a voice usually reserved for discussing my math grade. "But I'm leaving it up to you."

I didn't think twice. "I want to go."

Daddy looked disappointed, but all he said was, "The choice is yours."

I felt crummy disappointing Daddy. But he just didn't understand things, like first dates. And that a Negro would feel out of place at a white kids' party.

16

JACKSON DAILY JOURNAL, Friday, May 7, 1965

KKK MURDER TRIAL
ENDS IN HUNG JURY

★April crawled by, hot and sticky. Teachers shouted over the roaring floor fans at the front of the room. The end of school seemed a million days away. At least I had the Class Day party to look forward to.

The sixth grade talked of nothing else.

"Finally," said Saranne. "We're almost teenagers."

"You're only eleven," Carrie pointed out.

"I said *almost*." Saranne gave her the evil eye. "I mean, this is our first girl-boy party. I've got shoes with heels. And hose."

"Huh?" Cheryl blinked.

"Only a *baby* would wear *socks* to a party," Saranne said in a superior voice.

Great. Something else to argue about with Mama.

"All the girls are wearing nylons and shaving their legs for

Class Day," I told her. "I'll be the only one with hairy legs. Gross!"

"You can wear nylons," said Mama. "But I didn't shave my legs until I was seventeen."

"That was back in the Dark Ages," I wailed. "Things are different now."

"How are they different?" Mama could be *so* dense.

"Well, for one thing, skirts are a lot shorter."

"Okay," Mama agreed. "You can shave your legs next year in junior high."

"I'll be the only girl at the party with hairy legs. Jeb will be so embarrassed."

"Jeb better not be looking at your legs. End of discussion," said Mama.

"Sure, I'll show you how to shave your legs," said Pammie when I asked her. "My house or yours?"

"Mine." No way was I going to shave my legs in Jeb's house!

The night before Class Day, Pammie arrived after supper with a tote bag of giant curlers and Dippity-Do on top, a razor and a can of shaving cream on the bottom.

"I'm setting Alice's hair for Class Day," she explained to Mama.

"That's nice," said Mama, not looking up from the sinkful of supper dishes.

Pammie and I settled into the bathroom, the transistor turned up so Mama couldn't eavesdrop. Pammie quickly wound my hair on jumbo rollers before she got out the shaving stuff.

I stroked through the shaving cream, straight down my shin bone. A streak of pink lather followed the razor.

"Alice!" said Pammie. "You're supposed to stroke up, not down! Get some Band-Aids before you bleed all over the place."

The Band-Aids made a plastic racing stripe down the front of my leg. I hoped they wouldn't show through my new nylons.

Shaving was bad enough, but those nylons! It took me forever the next morning to get them on. I bunched the stocking in my hand the way Pammie showed me. My thumbnail poked through the sheer nylon. Rats! Fortunately, stockings came three pair to the box. I bunched and pulled another one over my Band-Aids. The Band-Aids showed. Chicken hips!

I snapped the garters to the stocking tops. The straps twisted and the nylons bagged around my ankles. I unsnapped the garters and yanked them up. Maybe being a teenager wasn't all it was cracked up to be.

Since the Class Day program was after school, the sixth-grade girls had a long, long day of tugging at hose through their skirts. Finally, the school day ended.

Miss Gruen pounded out "Pomp and Circumstance" on the piano as we marched into the auditorium past rows and rows of moms in flowered hats. No dads. Just moms. All the dads were at work.

All except Valerie's dad. Reverend and Mrs. Taylor sat in the front row, dressed like they were going to a fancy party instead of a grade-school graduation. I thought he would look different, after being in jail, but he looked the same as always. Solemn, in a suit and tie.

The sixth grade thumped up the stage steps to rows of folding chairs. The girls' new French heels clonked like wooden shoes. It was about a hundred degrees in the auditorium, even with the windows open. We blinked and yawned. Garter snaps dug into the backs of my legs as I squirmed on the metal chair.

Tommy led the prayer, which we couldn't hear since he prayed into his tie instead of the microphone. Skipper led the pledges to the American and Mississippi flags so fast he might as well have been speaking Russian.

Mr. Thibodeaux talked about what good neighbors and citizens we all had been this year. I guess he forgot about us putting gum in Valerie's hair.

We stood and recited "Hiawatha" together, sang "This Is My Country" and "Dixie." Carrie read a long, boring essay about some Confederate general. Mary Martha and Skipper won the Eleanora Parnell Good Citizen Award.

"Whyn't they just call it the Teacher's Pet Award," grumped Saranne.

The six best folk dancers did the "Mexican Serape Dance." I wasn't one of them. We sang a couple more songs, marched out to the "King Cotton March" (what else?), and that was it. Big deal.

The big deal was the party. Everybody was itching to get to the country club. But first, there were pictures.

All the moms had cameras and snapped about a million pictures. Pictures of us in front of the school. Pictures with our friends. I stood with the rest of the Cheerleaders on the front steps as each of our mothers took the exact same shot.

Pictures with our teachers. I tried to drag Miss LeFleur into one of my pictures.

"Sorry, Alice," she said, backing toward the parking lot. "I'm late for an engagement. Have a wonderful time at your party, dear." She trotted off on her high heels, White Shoulders perfume hanging in the air.

Nobody wanted to be in Valerie's pictures. She posed with her mom, then her dad, and finally Lucy. I felt sorry for her. I checked to see if anyone was watching before I went over to her.

"Great dress, Valerie. Where did you get it?" It was the prettiest in the class, white linen embroidered with lilies of the valley.

"New Orleans."

I didn't have to ask why she went all the way to New Orleans for a dress.

"Come along, Valerie," called Mrs. Taylor. "People are waiting for us at the house."

"Having a party?" I asked.

"Yes," said Valerie. "A graduation party for me. Bye."

So there, Daddy! Valerie's having her own party.

Cars started to leave for the country club. I spotted Jeb with his buddies, horsing around by the bike racks, their madras sport jackets flung on the grass.

"Hey there," I began, but Jeb cut me off.

"Not here," he said out of the corner of his mouth, like a TV gangster. He jerked his thumb toward the teachers' parking lot. I followed him around back. He reeked of Old Spice.

"Here's the rules," he said. "You walk behind me. Act like we're not together."

"That's not fair! You're supposed to be my date."

"Take it or leave it." Jeb marched off to the curb where the Mateers' car waited.

I followed, calling Jeb nine kinds of rat fink under my breath.

Some date! I climbed in the backseat. Jeb got in the front. He messed with the radio while Mrs. Mateer smoked and yakked about dances she had gone to when she was a girl.

"Leave us here, Mama," Jeb said as the car crunched into the gravel drive of the country club. He was halfway to the clubhouse before I was out of the car.

"Wait up," I yelled. I ran after him, and lost a shoe in the driveway gravel.

Chicken hips! I might as well have come by myself.

I jammed the shoe back on, and followed Jeb's madras sport jacket into the clubhouse.

Inside the ballroom, Mary Martha's cousin's band tuned up. If the Walloos knew Beatles songs, they sure weren't playing them. They played "Gloria," a song that had only three chords.

The singer would say, "We'd like to do the Beatles for you now," and play something you couldn't tell *what* it was. Then they'd play "Gloria" again.

The boys took turns sliding from one end of the waxed dance floor to the other in their sock feet. So did some of the girls, me included. No one was dancing. I wondered why everybody made such a big deal about coming with a date. Our dates didn't get near us all evening!

At ten o'clock the Walloos played "Goodnight, Sweetheart," a real old-fashioned slow-dance song. Everyone just stood around until Mary Martha's father hollered, "This is it, kids. Boys, dance with the young lady you came with."

Jeb came over, but stood about ten feet away.

"Hey, I won't explode," I hollered. Very slowly, he came closer. His shirt was sweaty, his jacket missing, and the Old Spice evaporated. I sure didn't want to touch him. "Do you know how to slow dance?"

"Nope." We looked around. Kids were dancing at arm's length, fingertips resting on the shoulders of their partner. So that's what we did. Not real romantic, but not gross either.

I wonder if Valerie is dancing at her party. I hope she's having fun.

I was happy to let Jeb and his sweaty shirt sit in the front seat going home.

Mama and Daddy were in the den watching Johnny Carson when I came in.

"Did you have a good time?" they asked at the same time.

My feet hurt and "Gloria" pounded in my brain.

"Yeah," I said. "I'll tell you all about it in the morning."

Only I didn't.

It seemed like I had just put my head on my pillow when . . .

Ka-boom. The windows rattled and my bed shook.

A bomb. Not in my neighborhood, but not far away.

I knew what would happen next. I watched the glowing second hand whir around the face of my clock radio. Nine minutes, ten minutes . . .

The phone rang. In my parents' room, Daddy said, "I'll be right there." He slammed the receiver down so hard the bell jingled.

"What is it now?" said Mama.

"Someone wired dynamite to Reverend Taylor's car over in Tougaloo."

"And . . ." Mama's voice trailed off.

"He's dead." The closet door creaked open. Hangers scraped the clothes rod.

I ran to my parents' room. Daddy had on pants and his pajama top. He yanked a clean shirt from a hanger.

"But what, but how . . ." I knew Daddy didn't have the answers. That wasn't what I wanted anyway. I wanted him to pat me on the back and say, "There, there, Pookie. It'll be all right."

Daddy buttoned his shirt. "Go back to bed, Alice."

I crawled under the covers, turned up my transistor, and cried. Cried for the little girl I'd never be again. Cried because Daddy couldn't make everything right.

And I cried for a girl who would never see *her* daddy again.

17

CIVIL RIGHTS LEADER'S FUNERAL TOMORROW
No Suspects in Car Bomb Slaying

★Monday was a beautiful morning. I wore a new outfit, a plaid blouse and skirt that matched the blue sky. New outfits usually made me feel like skipping, even if I was almost twelve. But not this morning.

The sixth graders stood in hushed knots on the playground, the usual groups broken and scattered. Boys stood with girls, the Cheerleaders here and there. Kids wandered from one cluster to another, checking rumors, adding to them.

"Our maid, Inez, says Martin Luther King is preaching at the funeral," said Jeb.

"I heard Reverend Taylor was blown to smithereens," contributed Andy.

Jeb turned to me. "Your daddy's FBI. What do you know?"

"You kidding? I haven't seen him since Friday night." Even if I had, Daddy never talked about work.

"Nigger had it coming to him." Leland lolled against the bike racks.

I waited for someone to say, "Shut up, Leland."

No one did. Including me.

"I heard his wife had him kilt," said Karla. "He was running around on her, so she paid to have his car blowed up."

Shut up, Karla.

I didn't say that either.

There had to be something I could do. But what? I was too chicken to even tell Karla and Leland to shut up.

The school doors banged open, the "King Cotton March" cranked up, and down the hall we marched. Left, right, left, right. Just like any other morning.

We said the Pledge and the Lord's Prayer. Any other morning.

Miss Gruen cleared her throat. "Boys and girls," she began. "I'm sure you've heard by now that Valerie's father was killed Friday night."

Outside, a motor scooter putt-putted by, birds chirped in the oak, the chains on the flagpole clanked in the breeze.

Inside 6B, silence.

"It's a small mercy that his family did not witness this tragedy."

Clank clank clank. The sound of the chains filled the room.

"The police are doing their best to find out who did this. Until they do, I will not tolerate gossip and rumor in my class-room." Miss Gruen gave us the Look over the top of her glasses. "Remember Valerie and her family in your prayers.

But there are three weeks left in this school year and we have work to do."

"Miss Gruen." Mary Martha raised her hand. "Aren't we going to take up money for flowers?"

"Nigger lover," Leland mumbled.

"Of course," said Miss Gruen. "Mary Martha, you take charge. Would someone else like to help?"

Something to help Valerie! I raised my hand and looked around.

Mine was the only hand up.

"Very well, Alice." Miss Gruen sounded like she wished someone else had raised their hand. Someone better in math.

"If everybody gives a quarter, that's more than eight dollars," said Mary Martha, figuring on her notebook cover. "We can get something nice for that."

"What for?" blurted out Saranne. "Why're we sending flowers to that nigra? If he hadn't gone around stirring up trouble, he wouldn't be dead."

"My daddy says he was a Commie," Debbie jumped in, without raising her hand.

"How could he be a Communist?" I didn't raise my hand either. "He was a minister. Communists don't believe in God."

"Class, this is exactly the sort of rumor and gossip I was talking about," Miss Gruen said. She rummaged in her desk and came up with a blank report-card envelope. "Put your contribution in here, if you wish. We will discuss this matter no further."

The envelope traveled up and down the aisles. A lot of kids passed it without opening it. I dropped in my quarter and shook the envelope. It felt awfully light.

"Seventy-five cents, three gum wrappers, and a baseball card," said Mary Martha after we counted the take during recess.

"What are we going to do?" I said. "That's not enough."

"I have three dollars," Mary Martha said. "I was going to get the new Beatles album, but I guess that can wait."

"I've got two dollars." It was my whole allowance for the next two weeks. "Can we get something for five dollars and seventy-five cents?"

"I don't know. I think six dollars is as cheap as flowers come."

I slid my two dollars into the envelope. That left me the two dimes Mama always made me carry in case of emergency. I wasn't supposed to spend it unless I had to.

"Did you girls collect enough money?" Miss Gruen asked after recess.

"No, ma'am," said Mary Martha. "Not quite."

"Let me add my donation," said Miss Gruen. She hauled an ancient pocketbook from the bottom desk drawer. From a leather change purse she handed us a dollar bill, worn soft as velvet. "Y'all take care of this during lunch."

As 6B filed down the hall to lunch, Mary Martha and I walked past the cafeteria and the office and through the front door. It felt weird being out of school in the middle of the day.

"We're going to Culver's," said Mary Martha, leading the way. "That's where Mama buys flowers. Mr. Culver knows me."

Culver's Florist was a Hansel-and-Gretel kind of house with red shutters and a picture window filled with roses. A mostly bald man in a gray smock slouched from the back room at the jingle of the screen-door bells.

"Why, Mary Martha Goode," he said. "Aren't you supposed to be in school?"

"Yessir, Mr. Culver. Our teacher knows we're here. A girl in our class, her daddy died, and we want to send flowers to the funeral."

"That's a shame." Mr. Culver settled his gold-rimmed glasses on his nose. "How much did you want to spend?"

"We only have six dollars and seventy-five cents," said Mary Martha, opening her purse.

"I can give you a nice spray of carnations for that," said the florist. "Red and white. Will that do?"

"Yessir, that sounds pretty." Mary Martha handed the florist the money. "Could we see them before you deliver them?"

"Why, surely. I'll have 'em waiting for y'all after school."

We jingled back out the screen door. My heart felt lighter. I'd done something for Valerie.

After school, I called Mama from the office to tell her where I was going.

"Mrs. Goode can bring me home," I said, since Daddy had the car. I hung up before Mama could think of more things to worry about.

Mary Martha and I walked back to Culver's. The tree shadows were deeper now, the air hot and thick with the scent of a hundred spring gardens.

"Where should we send the flowers?" Mary Martha asked.

"The newspaper said the viewing is at Harrison's Funeral Home on Pearl Street," I said as we pushed open Culver's screen door. "Viewing" was such a weird word for looking at a dead body. I was glad I wasn't going to the viewing.

"They're all ready," said Mr. Culver. He disappeared in back, returning with an armload of red and white carnations. "Now, where do y'all want this delivered?" Mr. Culver's pencil was poised over a delivery slip.

"Harrison's Funeral Home on Pearl Street," I said.

Mr. Culver's pencil still hovered in the air. Suddenly the room seemed too sunny. Too quiet.

"They're for Reverend Taylor's funeral," I explained.

The florist scowled. "I don't have time for foolishness, young lady. Mary Martha, where are these flowers going?"

"She's not fooling," she said. "Reverend Taylor's daughter is in our class."

"Do your folks know you're sending flowers to a dead nigger preacher?" The florist's face purpled, sun flaming off his gold-rimmed glasses.

"They do," said Mary Martha. "Will you please deliver them?"

"No, ma'am." Mr. Culver's jaw jutted. "I don't deliver in Niggertown."

"What are we going to do?" I asked.

"That's your problem." Mr. Culver tore up the delivery slip, shoved the carnations across the counter to Mary Martha, and marched us out the door. He slammed it so hard, the bells flew off the door spring.

We stood, dazed, in the afternoon heat. Mary Martha clutched the spray of flowers, looking for all the world as if she had just won a beauty contest.

"Now what?" she said.

18

THOUSANDS EXPECTED FOR TAYLOR FUNERAL
Martin Luther King to Lead Service

★Sun shimmered on something bright at the end of the block. Maids in white uniforms, waiting for the bus. The bus to the Negro neighborhoods.

"We'll deliver the flowers ourselves," I said. "I'll ask those maids which bus to take. C'mon."

I took a few steps before realizing Mary Martha and the flowers hadn't budged.

"Well, are you coming?" I asked.

"Are you *crazy*?" said Mary Martha. "Go to a colored funeral home? On a *bus*?"

"Well, yeah." What did she think would happen? "Why not?" Mary Martha stared into the carnations.

"Why not?" I repeated loudly. "You're not scared, are you?"

"I can't. I just can't," Mary Martha whispered.

"But you're a million times braver than me. You got Valerie her curtain call in the Christmas pageant. Remember?"

"That was different."

Voices crowded my head.

Mary Martha. *White people in a colored neighborhood. Who knows what could happen?*

Jeb. *Buses ain't for white people.*

And everyone else, over and over. *That's just the way things are. That's the way they've always been.*

I was mad. At Mr. Culver. At Mary Martha for finking out on me. At the stupid rules about white people and black people.

Time for *my* rules. The Alice Rules.

"Give me those flowers." I snatched them from Mary Martha. "I'll go by myself."

Mary Martha's eyes looked sad. I knew she *wanted* to come with me. She *knew* it was the Right Thing to Do. She just couldn't.

But I could. I was *mad*.

Mad enough to put one foot in front of the other all the way to the bus stop.

"Excuse me, does this bus go to Pearl Street?" The maids looked at each other, like this might be a trick question from a smart-mouth white girl. Finally, a young woman in beat-up Keds said, "Yeah. It go that way."

A green city bus roared up in a cloud of exhaust.

"Little girl?" said the driver as I dropped my emergency dime into the fare box. "Where do you think you're going?"

"Pearl Street." I sounded a lot cooler than I felt.

He eyed me and the flowers. "Do your mama and daddy know where you're going?"

"Yessir." What was he going to do? Call them up and ask?

The only empty seat was at the back. I staggered down the aisle, holding the flowers in front of me like a shield, passing seat after seat of uniformed maids. Were they whispering about me? Was I the first white person to ride a city bus?

Don't be chicken, Alice. Remember the Alice Rules.

A tall woman with reddish brown hair swayed down the aisle, clutching at the seat backs as she went. Inez Green, the Mateers' maid.

"Miss Alice?" Inez slid into the seat beside me. "Where you goin' with them flowers?"

I told her. I waited for her to say I was crazy. Or to ask if my mama knew where I was. She didn't.

"You know what stop to get off at?" she said.

"Pearl Street, wherever that is."

"I'll get off with you. I want to pay my respects to the Reverend myself. Now, less us open this window 'fore we smother to death."

The bus groaned through white neighborhoods, stopping every couple of blocks to take on more maids. Down Capitol Street, past Kennington's Department Store, the Paramount Theater, and the King Edward Hotel, then through the railroad underpass.

On the other side of the underpass, the world was all Negro.

Barbershops and beauty salons and a corner grocery with Negroes bustling in and out. We stopped at a red light. Through the open bus window, Junior Walker and the All Stars' "Shotgun" blared from a loudspeaker outside a record store. I didn't like that song. It began with a shotgun blast. I shivered, glad when the light changed.

We rode down narrow streets lined with unpainted shacks. Up streets with houses so bright and tidy they reminded me of birdhouses.

"Pearl Street," announced Inez, standing up. "We getting off here, Miss Alice."

Pearl Street didn't look like the other neighborhoods. Big old-fashioned houses with wide porches, set far back from tree-shaded curbs. Velvety, terraced yards. Sweet-smelling, big-headed hydrangeas drooped in the afternoon shadows.

"You sure this is the right street?" I asked.

"You tellin' me I don't know my own part of town?" Inez smiled, so I knew she wasn't mad. "This be where the doctors and lawyers live. There's well-off colored people, y'know. We ain't all dirt-poor."

Well-off colored people. It was something I'd never thought of. I knew Valerie wasn't dirt-poor. Her dresses were as nice as anyone else's in 6B. Her parents' station wagon was no fancier than our Chrysler. I figured Valerie probably lived in a house that looked a lot like mine. Not too big, not too small. Nothing like the houses on Pearl Street. These were big, old-fashioned two-story houses, with Cadillacs and Lincolns gleaming in the driveways.

At the end of the block sat the biggest house of all. A blue neon sign on the lawn announced HARRISON'S FUNERAL PARLOR, SINCE 1919. A stream of Negroes trudged up the terrace steps and into the house.

I felt very, very white, just like that day at the football game. Unlike that day, though, everyone was too sad to notice a white girl in school clothes carrying carnations.

Inez and I joined the line of mourners that snaked up the block. People in their Sunday best, hats and gloves, suits and ties. Men in overalls and uniformed maids coming from work. The line crept silently along. It was spooky, that many people, and nobody making a sound.

On the street, cars and pickup trucks crawled by, honking, Confederate flags snapping from radio antennas. Over the horns, white men and boys leaned out the windows, screaming. A long string of sounds, but I couldn't pick out words.

A mud-splashed truck pulled up to the curb. A teenager yelled out the window. "Hey, white girl. You lost?"

"Nah," shouted the driver, leaning across the boy. "She must be one of them nigger-loving Yankees." They hooted as they gunned the truck back into traffic.

More cars. More trucks. More screaming. Now I could tell what they were saying. White men screaming ugly words at the Negroes, who never looked up. Words hard and hateful enough to kill.

Then I knew. They weren't just words. Words show what's in your heart. Words spoken. And words unspoken.

All the words I left unsaid. Have to find Valerie. Tell her about the words.

The line slowed at the terrace steps, stretched up to the porch and into Harrison's. We shuffled forward. I was glad to be away from the street.

I had plenty of time to look around. News cameras rimmed the yard. Some white people stood on the lawn, smoking cigarettes and sipping from Dixie cups, as if this were a sad kind of garden party.

Inez nudged me. "Look over there."

I followed her gaze. A Negro man with a handsome round face leaned against a magnolia tree, talking to a shorter man with light brown curly hair.

"Sidney Poitier and Paul Newman," said Inez.

Reverend Taylor knew *movie stars?* Valerie never mentioned it. Valerie told us nothing.

We don't know you at all, Valerie.

A Negro girl and woman came down the porch steps, tears streaking their faces. Where had I seen them before? La Petite. The girl who wanted the pink lace dress. Today, she wore a white shift with daisies embroidered on the hem. I wondered where she bought it. New Orleans?

One step and another and we were on the porch. Two steps more brought us into the dim front hall. Fans on tall poles whirred in the corners, but they didn't help unless you were standing right under one.

I wasn't. My blouse was soaked with sweat, the skirt waistband limp and soggy. My hair stuck to my neck in damp strings. My sticky hands reeked of carnations. A blanket of smells smothered me: candle wax and furniture polish, hair pomade and a hundred clashing perfumes.

Valerie. Have to find Valerie.

At the head of the line stood a tall Negro gentleman in a dark suit. "You are here for . . . ?"

"We're here to see the Reverend," said Inez, as if she did this every day.

"Parlor two." The man waved us to the left, where even more people stood in line. "There are so many flowers, we are putting them in parlor three." He pointed to the other side of the hall.

The flower room was empty of people, late-afternoon sun slanting through the ruby-colored windowpanes. Empty of people, but floor-to-ceiling with flowers.

Roses and gladiolas and lilies and chrysanthemums. Wreaths with ribbons that said OUR FALLEN LEADER in glittery script. Sprays like ours, only bigger and fancier.

I tucked the carnations next to a gigantic basket of roses. The only bouquet smaller than ours was a bunch of garden flowers tied with package ribbon. "From the First Grade of Parnell School," said the card, manila drawing paper folded in half. I wondered how the first grade got *their* flowers here.

"Look a'here." Inez stood before a mass of calla lilies, a florist card dangling from her fingers. "From Marlon Brando, the actor. The Reverend sure did know a lot of famous folks."

I stuck my nose in the flowers. Calla lilies do not smell pretty. Something rotten lurked beneath the perfume. It made my head hurt.

Inez's eyes widened as she inspected a spray of white roses. "From President Johnson hisself," she whispered. Then she sort of shook herself and said, "We best be payin' our respects. Buses stop running out your way at six."

Back to the packed hallway. Sweat trickled down my back as bodies pressed me on all sides. The humming fans and moans from the viewing room jumbled together in a nightmarish way.

My stomach roiled. Black fishlike spots swam before my eyes. I had skipped lunch to buy the flowers.

I will not pass out.

"Child, you all right?" Inez flapped a hanky in my face. "You look like you fixin' to faint."

"I'm fine."

I will see Valerie. I will.

The line inched forward. I stared at the dusty toes of my shoes. The black fish spots went away, but my head still hurt. Cold sweat prickled the back of my neck.

Have to find Valerie. Tell her I'm sorry. Sorry for everything.

A familiar scent drifted over the stink of sweat and too many flowers. Yardley's English Lavender. A brown dress brushed past me.

"Miss Gruen?" Was I seeing things? "What are you doing here?"

Miss Gruen didn't look surprised to see me. "I am paying

my respects to a student who has lost her father." She smiled. I didn't know she even *knew* how to smile. "I'm happy to see you, Alice. It will comfort Valerie to know a classmate is here." Then she was gone, lavender scent trailing her.

A door creaked open, and men's voices mumbled. One, a little clearer than the rest, said, "I'll see if she can see you. No one will know you're here."

Men in dark suits elbowed past us. The crowd parted, and for a minute I saw Valerie, expressionless, in her beautiful white Class Day dress. She sat with her mother and Lucy next to the closed casket.

The men whispered with Mrs. Taylor, then started hustling people outside. Next thing I knew, Inez and I were back out on the porch.

"Y'all wait outside," said one of the men. "Some folks want to speak with Miz Taylor in private."

"What's going on?" I whispered to Inez.

"I 'spect some big shots is wantin' to see Miz Taylor without a bunch of people gawkin'. Maybe the vice pres'dent or Martin Luther King. Somebody like that." She squinted into the setting sun. "You need to be goin', child, if you want to make that last bus. Is there somethin' I can tell that little Taylor girl for you?"

"Sorry," I said as I turned toward the bus stop. "Tell her Alice Ann Moxley says she's sorry."

19

REVEREND TAYLOR BURIED
IN ARLINGTON CEMETERY

★Mama had a fit about my going to the funeral home, even after I explained about Mr. Culver and Mary Martha and Inez.

"What did I do wrong?" I asked over and over.

Mama couldn't tell me. All she said was, "All those screaming rednecks. So unpleasant." The news cameras hadn't just filmed movie stars.

I looked at Mama, and I didn't see just her. I saw a grownup who didn't know the answer and didn't know the question. Because she didn't want to. Because it was unpleasant. Mama never wanted to see anything unpleasant.

I felt sorry for Mama.

Reverend Taylor was buried in Arlington National Cemetery in Washington, D.C. I saw Valerie and her family on Walter

Cronkite with President and Mrs. Johnson at the White House. Valerie looked so sad, I bet she didn't even know where she was.

A couple of days later, Mary Martha brought a copy of *Life* to school.

"Look," she called, waving the magazine. "Look who's on the cover."

The sixth grade crowded around Mary Martha and *Life*. Valerie and her little sister were on the cover! Valerie's arm was around Lucy, who clutched a white Raggedy Ann doll.

Mary Martha riffled the pages until she found the story: SORROW IN MISSISSIPPI: CIVIL RIGHTS LEADER REVEREND CLAYMORE TAYLOR ASSASSINATED. It was mostly pictures from the funeral. Paul Newman and Sidney Poitier shaking hands with Mrs. Taylor. Martin Luther King preaching. The girl in the daisy dress hugging Valerie. The caption read "Daughter Valerie Irene is comforted by her cousin Demetria Taylor." So that's who that girl was.

The first bell shrilled across the playground. Mary Martha closed the magazine.

"I didn't know Valerie's middle name was Irene," I said as we lined up.

"There's a lot we don't know about Valerie." Mary Martha's eyes looked sad. "Alice, about not going with you that day . . ."

"S'okay," I mumbled.

"No, it's not okay," Mary Martha said firmly. "I let you down."

"I don't get it," I said. "I mean, the flowers were your idea in the first place."

Mary Martha swallowed hard before she answered. "You know, the only reason I took up that flower money was manners. It was poor manners not to."

"But wasn't it poor manners not to take them?"

Mary Martha gazed off across the street at a yardman on his knees, weeding a flower bed. "The thing about manners is they're easy. It's easier to be nice to people than nasty. If you're nice, people think you're a good person. But sometimes manners aren't enough, I guess."

"Yeah." Feeling brave, I said, "So when Valerie comes back, maybe we should try to be her friends? She's really nice when you get to talking to her."

"Friends? Us?" Mary Martha sounded scared. "It's not that easy, you know."

"Yeah, I know. But maybe if there are two of us being friends with her, it won't be so hard. Just think about it, okay?"

"Okay. I'll think about it." Mary Martha smiled. "We both need some new friends."

She had that right. If it weren't for Mary Martha, I could go a whole school day with no one speaking to me. Not even Jeb. I missed him.

Then one morning on the bus, he slid into the seat next to mine.

"Sorry I've been such a goob," he said, staring at the back of Ralph's head.

"Oh yeah? What changed your mind?" He wasn't getting off that easy.

"Inez. She gave me what-for. Said riding that bus by your-self was the bravest thing she'd ever seen a white person do. She also said she wasn't making pimiento cheese until I apol-ogized."

We looked at each other, then burst out laughing. I knew it wasn't the pimiento cheese; Jeb really *did* think I was brave. That was better than wearing his ID bracelet. Well, almost.

I wasn't the only one in trouble over Reverend Taylor's fu-neral.

"Mama says Miss Gruen has lost her mind, going to a nig-ger funeral," said Saranne.

"My daddy said the same thing." Debbie flipped her sheep-dog bangs out of her eyes. "Says public schools is going to the niggers. He's sending me to Council School next year."

Other classmates would not be going on to Belson Junior High. Skipper's daddy was sending him to military school in Alabama.

"All that marching and saluting. Might as well join the army and get it over with," Skipper griped.

No one was surprised when Leland announced he was go-ing to Council. Karla said she wanted to, but her parents couldn't afford it.

"I reckon I'll be stuck going to school with niggers forever," she grouched.

And I'd be stuck with Karla and her fingernails forever. I hoped she'd find someone else to torture in seventh grade.

Junior-high orientation was the last day of school. The sixth graders would ride the bus over to Belson to get our schedules and lockers and find the rest rooms. Could anything bigger possibly happen in our lives?

Something did, the Sunday before orientation.

"Alice, would you bring in the paper?" Mama asked as I staggered out to the kitchen. I hated getting up early, but Sunday school started at nine.

"I'm not dressed." I poured myself a bowl of Cocoa Krispies.

"You've got your robe and slippers on." Mama sipped her coffee. "Who's going to see?"

A lot of people. Namely, Jeb.

"How come Daddy didn't bring in the paper?" Usually Daddy finished the crossword puzzle before I got out of bed.

"Because he came in very late. Big arrests last night. Now, scoot."

The paper lay at the end of the driveway in the storm gutter. I hoped I could grab it and hurry back inside before anyone saw me.

I clutched my nylon robe, which was missing buttons, scurried down the drive, and snatched up the paper. The flimsy rubber band holding the rolled paper snapped, and paper sections exploded all over the yard.

"Rats, rats, rats," I muttered as I gathered the sports and comics and want ads. Last, I picked up the front news section.

That's when I saw Miss LeFleur. Two pictures. Dead center of the front page.

The headline: TEACHER ARRESTED IN KLAN RAID: BEING HELD IN TAYLOR SLAYING.

I forgot to hold my robe shut. Forgot who might be watching. Forgot about breakfast and Sunday school. I stood in the driveway and read about Miss LeFleur.

The first picture was from her college yearbook. It looked just like her; hair in a perfect flip, a string of pearls around her neck.

The other picture . . . well, if the paper hadn't said it was Miss LeFleur, I wouldn't have guessed. She was flanked by two policemen gripping her upper arms. Her hair was all messed up. She crooked her elbow over her face so no one would recognize her. I did. I recognized her charm bracelet.

Even with the bracelet, it was hard to tell. This woman wore tight short-shorts with an equally tight short-sleeve sweater. The sweater was pulled up and you could see her belly button. Miss LeFleur's belly button!

I read on. Miss Claudia LeFleur had been arrested with her boyfriend (Miss LeFleur had a boyfriend?) and a car full of dynamite. They had been caught wiring it to a Negro church. In her purse was a KKK membership card and a list of other places they'd planned to bomb. More churches, civil rights leaders. FBI agents. The police had found a map in their car. A map plotting the way to Tougaloo. Where Reverend Taylor was killed.

The paper drooped in my hand. I spied a plaid bathrobe at the end of the driveway next door. Jeb.

"Whaddya think of this?" he called, waving his paper. We walked toward each other, meeting by the Mateers' pine tree.

"But Miss LeFleur was so nice," I burst out.

"Yeah," Jeb said. "She don't seem the type to blow folks up."

All year I had told myself that bad people were easy to spot. They were stupid like Leland, or mean like Karla. But Miss LeFleur was a grown woman. A teacher. Nice to everybody.

Everybody but Valerie. I remembered the Lysol in Miss LeFleur's desk. *She don't mean anything by it,* Jeb had said.

But she had.

The ground shifted beneath my feet, as if there had been an earthquake. I knew there hadn't been. Only in my heart.

Jeb and I suddenly realized we were standing in the middle of the yard in our nightclothes and looked away from each other.

"Reckon I need to get ready for Sunday school." Jeb refolded his paper.

"Yeah, me, too." I looked at the paper again. There was another story under the first one, interviews of people who knew Miss LeFleur. Some went to Miss LeFleur's church. They said she was a fine Christian. Sang in the choir. Never missed a Sunday.

She was missing this Sunday.

20

TEACHER ARRAIGNED
IN TAYLOR DEATH

★I pasted the headline in my scrapbook on the next-to-last page. One more page to fill, and the book would be finished.

I looked at the red fake-leather book with the word MEMORIES in curly gold letters on the front. I looked again at the picture of Miss LeFleur being arrested.

Keeping a current-events scrapbook was such a kid thing to do.

When this one was full, I wouldn't start another.

"All your fault, Yankee Girl." Karla's nails dug into my wrist. "If your FBI daddy stayed up North where he belonged, ain't none of this woulda happened. Miss LeFleur was framed by them nigger-loving Commies."

Jeb galloped over to the rescue. "Hey, Karla. Go pick on somebody as ugly as you are."

Karla let go of my wrist. "Take your old nigger-loving girl-friend, Jeb Mateer."

I rubbed the half-moon nail marks.

"Oh shut up, Karla," said Jeb.

Karla shot him the bird finger and stomped off.

"Stay away from her, y'hear?" Jeb gave me a warning look. "I ain't gonna bail you out all the time, y'know."

Monday, Tuesday.

I waited for Valerie to come back to school.

I'll make it up to you, Valerie. I'll be your friend.

Wednesday, Thursday. Still no Valerie. At least I had Orientation Day to take my mind off stuff.

"Orientation is a big deal. You want to look good, but like you could care less," Pammie told me. "Get it?"

I didn't, so Pammie went through her closet, looking for just the right outfit.

"Not bad at all." She studied me in her white hip-hugger skirt and turquoise-striped shirt with matching polka-dot necktie. "Now, if we could just do something with your hair."

I flipped through a *16 Magazine*. "Why can't my hair look like this?" I showed her a picture of Jane Asher.

"Because you don't iron your hair," said Pammie.

"You mean like with an iron and an ironing board? Should I?" I couldn't imagine Jane Asher running a steam iron over her long red hair.

"Nah, your hair's too short. You'd just wind up ironing your ears." Pammie squinted at me again. "You need hair straightener. They have do-it-yourself kits down at the Tote-Sum."

So that's what I did. I blew two weeks' allowance on a box of Straight and Swingy that Pammie put on for me. She left it on too long and cooked my head, but it didn't turn out half bad. I didn't look like Jane Asher, but I didn't look gross, either.

Friday and Orientation Day arrived. Decked out in Pammie's outfit and my straight if not swingy hair, I marched into 6B for the last time. The bulletin boards were bare, chalkboards washed, our *New Directions in Math* workbooks dumped in the giant trash barrel behind the cafeteria. Miss Gruen had packed away the odds and ends from her desk. This was her last day at Parnell, too.

Last day or not, Miss Gruen looked the same as ever. Old-lady lace-up shoes, brown dress, and a necklace that looked like watermelon seeds.

I knew I should say something to her, but what? I couldn't say "It's been fun," because it hadn't. I couldn't say "I really liked having you for a teacher," because I hadn't. I guessed I'd just say "Thank you, ma'am." And really mean it. She'd like that. Especially the "ma'am" part.

I looked around the room. So many empty desks of kids who wouldn't be going with us.

Tommy, whose daddy had a new church in Tupelo. Leland, who was going to Council with Debbie. Andy, who to Jeb's disgust decided to follow Debbie.

"Council don't even have a football team," Jeb argued.

Skipper came flying through the door just as the tardy bell rang.

"Thought you were going to that military school," said Saranne.

"Talked Daddy out of it," he panted as he landed in his seat. "Told him Belson had a better football team."

For the last time 6B said the Pledge and the Lord's Prayer. Miss Gruen cleared her throat.

Uh-oh. Lecture time.

"It has been quite a year," she began. "I hope we are all better citizens than we were in September."

From across the room I caught Mary Martha's uncomfortable look.

Come back, Valerie. I'll be a better citizen. Promise.

Miss Gruen was still talking. "I know you're all concerned about Valerie."

"Yeah, right," muttered Saranne.

Miss Gruen didn't hear her. "Valerie will not be returning. The Taylors have moved to New York City to be near relatives."

New York City!

Valerie was gone for good.

But I never got to say I'm sorry. Never got to be her friend.

I hardly noticed when the bus arrived and we all trooped on. I stared out the bus window. I had messed up so many things in the sixth grade. I'd probably mess up seventh grade, too.

"Scoot over." Mary Martha plopped down next to me. "Maybe they'll change their minds and move back," she said, reading my thoughts.

"Yeah, right." Now I sounded like Saranne.

"Well, they might," said Mary Martha, but not like she really meant it. We sat in silence, unable to think of anything cheerful to say. Finally, Mary Martha reached into her wicker purse and pulled out a transistor. "Now that Debbie's gone, I guess I'll have to bring the music." She clicked it on.

The Supremes, singing "Come See about Me."

"What station do you have on?" I asked.

"Rebel Radio, what do you think?" said Mary Martha. We listened, smiling. If Rebel Radio could play the Supremes, maybe things *could* change. Just maybe.

Carrie sat alone across the aisle, staring into a compact mirror, fluffing her face with a blusher brush. Alone? I leaned across Mary Martha and jogged Carrie's elbow.

"Hey, Carrie, what gives? How come you aren't sitting with the Cheerleaders?"

"Oh them," Carrie sniffed. "I'm sick to death of ol' Saranne telling me what to do. Saying I was weird for liking Ringo. Who made her boss? She isn't even a cheerleader anymore. At Belson, kids vote on cheerleaders."

I glanced at Saranne in the rear seat. She looked lost with only Cheryl for company.

Mary Martha followed my gaze. "I've known Saranne since kindergarten. I never thought she'd turn out so downright mean. People sure aren't what they seem sometimes."

"Yeah," I said. "Like Miss LeFleur." Thinking hard made me want to chew on something. "Got any toothpicks?" I asked.

"You kidding?" said Mary Martha. "Toothpicks are out. Binaca is in."

She fished in her purse again, pulled out what looked like a lipstick tube, and uncapped it. "Open wide," she ordered. I did. She squirted something peppermint into my mouth.

"What is that?" I asked, once I got the feeling back in my tongue.

"Spray mouthwash," she said, helping herself to a few squirts. "Much cooler than toothpicks. Besides," she lowered her voice, "you never know when a boy is going to kiss you. In junior high, you always have to be prepared."

Kissing? And all I had been worried about was being late to class.

The bus pulled up to Belson. I had seen it a zillion times, but it had never seemed so huge before.

"I hear they make seventh-grade girls use the rest rooms on the third floor," announced Saranne. "If an eighth or a ninth grader catches you in the other rest rooms, they flush your head."

"Gross!" said Cheryl.

"Oh hush, Saranne," said Mary Martha without turning around. "That's a rumor the ninth graders start every year. They just want to see if the stupid little seventh graders will believe it."

Saranne opened her mouth, then closed it. And sat back. And hushed.

Belson's principal stood on the front steps, speaking into a bullhorn. "You are divided by last name. Look for your letter group. Pick up your schedule," he bellowed over and over.

Long folding tables were set up on the lawn. Signs taped to the tables said A–G, H–M, and so on.

"Guess we split up for a while," said Mary Martha. "See you at lunch, okay?"

"C'mon, Alice," said Jeb. "Let's see if we can find our way around." He socked me on the shoulder as we got in line. I wondered if seventh-grade boys were more mature than sixth-grade ones.

So our first official act of junior high was lining up. I thought I'd left lines behind at Parnell. I kind of expected to hear the "King Cotton March."

There must have been three hundred kids milling around, all white except for a handful of Negro kids. A Negro girl in a green-flowered shift and pointy-toed flats wandered past our line. She looked familiar.

"Stay away from that girl," I could hear Saranne mutter from the N–S line. "They wear them pointy shoes so they can kick you in a fight."

The girl didn't look like she wanted to fight. She looked lost and a little scared. Now, where had I seen her before . . .

"Name," said a disgustingly cheerful teacher at the head of the H–M line. His name tag said "Mr. Henderson."

"Alice Ann Moxley."

"Moxley. Is that with an 'x'?" Not only was he way too happy first thing in the morning, but he had gooby glasses and a greasy flattop. He shuffled through a pile of papers.

"Yessir." More paper shuffling before Mr. Henderson handed me a schedule and a name tag. "I'll be your guidance counselor for the next three years. Any problems, just come to me. My office is room 101. I hope we'll be friends. Everybody calls me Uncle Jerry."

Uncle Jerry! Yeesh! I hated adults who tried to be your buddy. I wouldn't set foot in room 101 even if the entire ninth grade tried to flush me.

"Put on your name tag, Alice Ann Moxley," said Uncle Jerry. "We're all one big happy family here at Belson."

Oh yeah? I could already see cliques forming out on the lawn. Some new, some left over from their old schools. Skipper and Jeb stood with what looked like the football team. Saranne and Cheryl huddled alone by the empty bike racks. I didn't see Mary Martha at all.

The rest of the morning was as blurry as the carbon-copy schedule Uncle Jerry gave me. My classes must have been put together by a distance runner. English on the first floor, math on third, then PE on first, then back up to third for science.

At noon we were herded to the basement cafeteria for lunch. I took my pinkish hot dog and bun and found Mary Martha. She was sitting with Skipper.

"Siddown," said Skipper. "Pretty cool not having assigned seats, huh? Same old slop, though."

"Shove over," said Jeb, plunking his tray down. "This is so boss. We can talk without teachers getting on our case."

"Where *are* the teachers?" I asked. "I don't see any."

"Pammie says they eat in the teachers' lounge," said Jeb. "They take turns watching us. There's our warden for the day."

He pointed to Uncle Jerry, grinning like an idiot, oblivious to kids fork-flinging peas at him.

The four of us poked at our plates, trying to find something edible.

"I met this guy in PE who's going out for football," said Jeb, forking up Tater Tots. "Man, can he run. Pass, too. Name's Eddie Thigpen."

"You mean that colored kid you were horsing around with?" Skipper sounded surprised.

Jeb swallowed his mouthful. "Yeah. I mean, we got to talking football and . . ."

Suddenly, the room got quiet. Coming out of the lunch line was the Negro girl in the green dress. Then it hit me. She was Valerie's cousin Demetria.

I stood up.

"You going over?" whispered Mary Martha.

I nodded.

"You ain't gonna ask her to sit with us?" said Skipper, not whispering.

"You wanna make something out of it?" I said.

This is for you, Valerie.

Skipper swallowed the rest of his hot dog and grinned. "Nope. 'Cause I'm finished." He still had a nearly full tray. "Anybody else finished?"

Mary Martha gave him a dirty look but went on eating.

"How 'bout you, old buddy?" He flicked a pea at Jeb. Jeb glanced up from his Tater Tots.

I didn't wait to see what Jeb did. Or Skipper or Mary Martha.

I walked up to the girl in green. She stood in the middle of the room, gripping her tray. It was so quiet it was like being underwater.

Suddenly it was last September all over again.

Only this time, I'm getting it right.

"Hi. You're Valerie's cousin, aren't you?"

The girl flinched, as if I might hit her. Then she glanced at my name tag, and her face cleared. "Alice Ann Moxley. Ain't you the one they call Yankee Girl?"

"Yankee Girl, yeah, that's me," I said with a big fake smile. All around me kids muttered "Nigger lover, nigger lover" like a bunch of locusts.

Don't you be a chicken, Alice Moxley. Remember the Alice Rules.

"Valerie told me to watch for you," said Demetria.

I smiled for real. "Yeah?" What else was there to say? "C'mon, let's eat," I said as we walked back to our table.

Mary Martha and Jeb were still there.

AUTHOR'S NOTE

When I was ten years old, I knew three things were true:

1. Paul McCartney was the cutest Beatle, and the Beatles were the fabbest band in the whole world.
2. No matter how much Dippity-Do I used, my hair wasn't ever going to look like Jane Asher's, Paul McCartney's girlfriend.
3. And I would never live to see eleven. The Ku Klux Klan would shoot me, or burn our house, or blow up our car. I just knew it.

Like Alice, I was the daughter of an FBI agent. In the summer of 1964, my family moved from Chicago to Jackson, Mississippi. My father was one of 150 special agents ordered to Mississippi by President Lyndon Johnson.

Earlier that summer, three young civil rights workers disappeared near Philadelphia, Mississippi, where they were involved in registering African Americans to vote. At that time, white Southerners made it extremely difficult for black people to vote. College students and other concerned citizens from all over the country flocked South to help correct this situation. Southerners resented these "outsiders." The Ku Klux Klan did everything they could to intimidate the civil rights workers, including murder. The local law enforcement turned a blind eye to the Klan's activities. In some cases, law enforcement officers were members of the Klan themselves.

It was the disappearance of the three civil rights workers that moved President Johnson to order the FBI to Mississippi. Two months after they vanished, the FBI found the bodies of the three missing men, buried in an earthen dam. This was only the first of many cases to come of civil rights workers beaten or killed as they helped others become voting citizens.

These incidents took place forty years ago. When I tell people, particularly young people, about events that happened during my childhood, they find them hard to believe. "These things didn't *really* happen, did they?" they ask.

Oh, but they did. I knew I had to write about Mississippi in 1964. I didn't want people to forget that once there was a time, not so long ago, when African Americans could be treated so cruelly. Could be called horrible names like "nigger" and "coon." Could be *killed* for trying to vote. Or simply for looking a white person in the eye.

So while this is Alice's story, a lot of the things that happened to Alice also happened to me. My mother once said, "You know, someday you'll be glad you lived in this time and this place. You are seeing history in the making. You can tell your children and grandchildren about it."

She was right.